BRANKSOME LIBRARY
212-220 ASHLEY ROAD
POOLE BH14 9BY
Telephone: 01202 748832
Email: branksomelibrary@poole.gov.uk

Please return this item to any Poole library
by the due date.
Renew on (01202) 265200 or at
www.boroughofpoole.com/libraries

Dedication

I'd like to dedicate this book firstly to my family, Mum, Kev and Mark. For the great ideas, the encouragement and simply for being you. You are all my inspiration and this book would not have happened without you. You have my eternal gratitude and I love you all.

To my dad and the so called "Starmer humour" which I'm holding mainly responsible for the silliest of jokes within this book. I'm only so sad that you never got to read it, but I know how proud you would have been.

And of course to Lee for believing in me. Your endless optimism is both admirable and infectious and your support has kept me and this book going. For that I can never thank you enough. I love you with all my heart.

Huge thank you also to Hannah my best friend and number one fan (after my mum of course!) Your friendship and support means the world, just as much now as it did when we became friends in primary school. Also to my friend and very talented, patient hairdresser Sammie Coyle who beautifully styled my hair for my cover photo!

Finally to the rest of my friends and family that have contributed in their own little way, and to everyone else in my life. You are all Nutters and this book could not exist without you.

Kate Starmer

THE NUTTERS

Tiddles, Riddles & the Poisonous Poet

AUSTIN MACAULEY
PUBLISHERS LTD.

A CIP catalogue record for this title is available from the British Library.

ISBN 978 1 84963 956 9

www.austinmacauley.com

First Published (2015)
Austin Macauley Publishers Ltd.
25 Canada Square
Canary Wharf
London
E14 5LB

Printed and bound in Great Britain

Introduction

Once upon a time in the quaint village of Little Wobble there lived some Nutters. Albert and Primrose Nutter to be precise. Albert and Primrose (or Rose as she liked to be called) lived in a lovely little cottage with an impeccably kept front garden.

Rose is a large cuddly sort of woman with a very pretty and happy face. She has lovely dark straight hair and big bright eyes that seem to have a constantly excited twinkle about them. Also Rose is an avid gardener who enjoys making sure her plumage is better kept than Marjorie Floppington's next door. Rose also works part time from home for the local newspaper the Daily Wobble as an agony aunt under the pseudonym "Dear Doris". Unfortunately however the letters she gets tend to sway more towards the "Dear Doris, how can I get my pansies to flower all year round?" Rather than the more interesting "Dear Doris, I seem to have managed to get my girlfriend AND her mother pregnant, what should I do?" which would make her job much more interesting!

Albert, Rose's husband is a very bored insurance salesman. Albert used to be a policeman which he enjoyed very much, but sadly had to leave the force after getting stabbed in the leg by a clown (no joke). Turned out to be a multiple murdering clown no less! The clown, with the very unfunny name of Colin Killoran, had kidnapped three single mothers and their children, killing the mothers in his basement as and when he chose, and locking the children in a huge child's paradise toy room he had created in his attic. Albert had been the one to finally stop him and was lucky to escape with just the loss of his job. Fortunately he slept better knowing Colin the clown was well and truly locked up and had been for almost seven years now.

Albert, like his wife is large and cuddly. He has a kind round face, stubble on his chin and could be described as a gentle giant except that he might kill you if you call him that!

The Nutters have three children, Harry, Poppy and Charlie. Harry, the eldest is at university in the town of Appleleaf. Appleleaf is far enough away that he can act like he has left home but close enough that he can pop home to borrow money off his parents. Harry you see is an art student (a dosser and waste of space according to his father). He is a tall handsome boy with fairly long wavy hair that for some reason unbeknownst to his mother, girls find attractive. He may be a lazy bum but he can talk any girl into posing nude for his art projects (which incidentally is the only time his father takes an interest in his oldest son's schooling!)

Poppy is 18 and is at college. In daddy's eyes Poppy is his sweet baby darling daughter. In her mother's more knowing eyes however Poppy is a strikingly beautiful girl who while academically does very well she has all the common sense of a drunken pheasant. She is a tall slender girl with very long copper coloured hair and her mother's sparkly mischievous eyes. She has a part time job working in the local village pub "The Wobble Inn" which she thoroughly enjoys even though her boss Nigel the landlord can't even speak to her without dropping a glass and drooling much to the disgust of the landlady, Nigel's wife Felicity – more on these two later!

The youngest, Charlie is 15 and currently going through his GCSEs. Charlie like his older brother is a handsome boy but very shy. He has black square rimmed spectacles and much to the amazement of both his parents, a mega huge brain. Charlie is without a doubt in his father's eyes, "the milkman's". For his huge brain however Charlie is extremely clumsy and has had size 11 feet since he was 12 which he often trips over, usually when an attractive young lady is walking past. These things just tend to happen to Charlie.

The last member of the family to mention is the Nutter's beautiful but stupid Great Dane, Allan. Allan is a huge lazy lovable sort of creature who would rather lie in the sunshine in the garden all day than go "walkies" like any normal dog.

Albert is often seen dragging him up the garden path which it should be said is no easy feat for a dog of Allan's size. He has however been trained by his father to spring to life and look as big and terrifying as possible whenever a young man knocks the door for Poppy.

For all their good and bad points, the Nutters are a happy, almost normal sort of family.

After the nasty clown stabbed Albert in the leg and ended his all too short police career, Albert became, to put it mildly, cranky. Forced to give up the job he loved, serving the community, catching baddies and not to mention how much Rose fancied him in his uniform, he had taken a job in insurance. Claims to be precise. He was still able to do some mini detective work such as discovering the fraudulent claims. He once had a man try to claim life insurance on his dead wife only to discover that his wife was not dead at all but had run off to Spain with the next door neighbour and another that was actually caught on CCTV setting fire to his own warehouse. He would always come home from work and say to Rose, "If we could arrest people for being stupid we would have more people in prison than out!"

Anyway poor Albert massively missed his police career and no amount of insurance detective work would help make him happy.

It was one day when, after a particularly dull day at work, Albert had come through the front garden gate, pushed over one of Rose's favourite garden gnomes and accidentally on purpose trod on a defenceless snail, that Rose had the idea.

"Why don't we start a private detective business?" Rose had said. "It must be the next best thing to police work and you can work from home, choose your own hours and clients, and we can all help!"

After firstly poo poo-ing the idea Rose talked Albert into at least thinking about it, and that he did for at least the next twelve minutes over a large glass of red. The more wine he drank and the more Rose chatted on in the background about "helping the community" and "catching wives sleeping with the pool boy". The fact that his glass of red wine soon became a bottle and him admitting that his wife generally got her own way anyway he actually started coming round to the idea.

And so it was done.

A NUTTER &
P NUTTER LTD.

Private Detective Agency

No Job Too Small,
Call Today on 01234 007007

This is a story about some Nutters.

Chapter 1

Like all amazing new ideas they often, when put into practice, can be rather a let-down. Albert wanted to catch criminals and cheating spouses but instead had a string of milk bottle snatchers, nosy neighbours and hypochondriacs.

Mrs Jones had contacted Albert after Hilda next door hadn't been seen since last Tuesday and she was terribly worried that she might have had a fall or collapsed at home and was rotting away as we speak. Turns out Hilda had gone for a dirty weekend to Torquay with Harold the postman and wanted nobody to know especially "that nosy cow next door, Mrs Jones". Albert promptly reported to the nosy cow next door that Hilda had simply been "visiting family" and would next time leave her a note. CASE SOLVED.

Mrs Jones had also employed Albert to locate her stolen car as the police for some reason would not take her seriously. Turns out, after speaking to his old police buddy Dave that Mrs Jones didn't drive nor did she even own a car and apparently she was a "regular fruit loop".

"She's always down the station complaining about something or other the bloody nutter," Dave said.

"You sure she's not related to you," he laughed. Albert and Dave always had friendly funny banter especially about their names. Dave Ramsbottom should know better than to poke fun at other people's names Albert liked to point out. Albert decided to take Mrs Jones with a pinch of salt after that, and Rose said he had to stop charging her too as it was not right to bill loonies even the annoying time wasting ones.

Mr Green had also asked the Nutters to locate his missing garden gnome that was his pride and joy especially as "that old codger over the road, Mr Brown," was particularly jealous of Mr Green's award winning garden. 'Daily Wobble in Bloom - Best Kept Lawn' 2008, 2009 and 2010 to be precise! It didn't take Albert long (just a step ladder to look into Mr Brown's garden in fact) to discover who the mystery thief was and the fact that Mr Brown's lawn had won second place all those years was even more incriminating. CASE SOLVED. It was all just too much excitement for Albert and Rose.

Mrs Watkins had asked the Nutters to locate her precious cat "Tiddles" who had not been seen in over a week. The more Albert heard her describe the beautiful tortoiseshell moggy he couldn't help but think of the uncanny resemblance that Tiddles had to the cat he had to scrape off his front tyre earlier that very day. CASE UNSOLVED

"Someone must have cat napped beautiful Tiddles," he told Mrs Watkins. "Perhaps it's time to look for a new cat."

*

It was a dark and stormy evening in the quaint village of Little Wobble. A storm was raging outside, so loud in fact that Albert had to turn the TV up quite a lot in order to hear what was going on in the local news. Rose was just finishing the washing up when a roar of thunder made her jump and drop the plate she was drying right on the dog Allan's head. Allan had decided to go for a lie down in the middle of the kitchen floor which, when your dog is a bloody Great Dane like Allan, is rather inconvenient as he takes up almost the entire kitchen.

"Oh Allan you poor poor doggy woggy!" said Rose as she fell to the floor to inspect his skull and give him cuddles.

"Mummy is sorry Allan, what a clumsy Mummy." Incidentally Allan had barely opened one eye when said plate hit him on the head but decided to give Rose sad eyes so he could get a treat.

"Does Mummy's baby want a treat?" asked Rose apologetically. Rose treated Allan like he was her baby, much to Albert's dismay and refused to believe that Allan was "Just a dog".

After Albert assured Rose that there was no need to take Allan to the hospital and that Allan didn't have concussion, or need counselling, Albert and Rose flopped down on the sofa, Albert with a beer and Rose with a nice glass of wine.

The rain was continuing to hammer on the windows when there was a tap on the front door.

"Who the bloody hell is that at this hour?" Albert said.

"Well I don't know, I'm not expecting anyone, go answer it," replied Rose.

"I don't want to answer it, what if it's a mad axe murderer!"

"So you would happily send me to the door to answer it to the mad axe murderer would you?!" said Rose, getting up off the sofa.

"Charming! Well I hope it is a mad axe murderer now, then you'd feel guilty wouldn't you!"

"Well at least I'd be able to have the bed all to myself," replied Albert jokingly. Fortunately his wife had a sense of humour. "She had to have," he kept telling himself, "she married me." He smiled.

Rose went to answer the door. Albert could hear the mutterings of voices from the hallway for a few moments.

"If it's another one of those religious nuts tell him we're Satanists and he has interrupted our traditional Wednesday evening sacrifice of a goat or virgin whichever is easier to get hold of, probably the goat in this village," Albert half shouted half chuckled towards the hallway. Rose rolled her eyes but had a discreet smirk to herself. As she cautiously turned the old brass handle on her wooden cottage door a huge crash of thunder made her gasp and the lightning revealed the silhouette of a huge terrifying mad axe murderer, she knew it! Albert would probably turn the TV up as her screams would make it difficult for him to hear what was happening on Illicit Relations their favourite soap and the love triangle between Jack, his twin sister Jacquie and the intriguing Italian Isabella who they both madly love (but is actually a man) and now the mad axe murderer is at the door she will never know what happens!

When Rose returned a few moments later looking a little flustered (Albert was now talking about sacrificing Allan to the devil as he isn't much use for anything else) she was followed into the lounge by their best pals Dave Ramsbottom and his wife Sandra (who incidentally were not mad axe murderers, just mad.) Turned out the rather perfect axe silhouette had been a combination of Sandra's new bouffant hairdo and her fighting with the umbrella on the doorstep. Somehow Dave had already made it to the fridge and back armed with a beer himself (usual procedure) and Rose had whipped up a wine glass and was pouring Sandra a glass before they even had their coats off!

After exchanging the usual pleasantries, and the obvious sign that Sandra would in fact burst if she did not get it off her chest what she had actually came round for.

"Come on then Sand what's on your mind?" Albert laughed. "You look like you might actually explode all over my couch if you don't speak right away!"

"Gosh I'm glad you asked!" she blurted out. "Hold on to your hats Nutters, have I got an actual private detective case for you or what!" Sandra said in a very excitable voice. Sandra was quite a slim attractive lady for her age, always had a different hairdo every time Albert and Rose saw them. She always wore lots of makeup most of it on her teeth and tried ever so hard to sound posh when she was in fact from the east end of London. Dave had swept her off her feet as a keen young policeman from her abusive first husband and they had never looked back. Dave and Albert both met in the police when they were in their 20s and had been the best of friends ever since.

"Really?!" said Rose as excited as Sandra

"Really?" said Albert as excited as Allan the dog. Albert was always a tad sceptical about some of the things that came out of Sandra's mouth.

"Well, Rose, you know Shirl's friend Denise's mum's sister Vera who works down the post office?"

"Is Vera the one with the limp, a bit deaf?" said Rose instantly.

"No that's Wendy, Vera's the one who talks like she's sucking a boiled sweet, bald patch," Sandra said pointing to her huge bouffant.

"Oh of course I know Vera, actually bumped into her in the corner shop the other day when I was buying emergency sausages for Albert's tea 'cos Allan accidentally ate his steak which I left on the side," said Rose winking at Allan who could barely be bothered to open one eye to acknowledge his mummykins.

"What?! You gave my steak to that bloody lazy dog?" Albert began to say

"Shhh Albert, Sandra is talking," said Rose quickly changing the subject. "You were saying Sand?"

"Yes, well, Vera's got a twin who believe it or not works in the post office in Upper Wobble, I know what are the odds right?!"

"When you say twin, do you mean identical or different cos those twins in Charlie's class at school reckon they are identical but one of them has ginger hair and the other one is really good at sport," said Rose.

"No they aren't identical, Vera and George look nothing alike," said Sandra.

"Does it actually matter?" said Albert in disbelief.

"Anyway, George, Vera's twin brother is married to a woman called Mary who is extremely good friends with the Reverend Goodsoul's wife Patricia."

Albert and Dave looked at each other like their wives were talking in code.

"And now for the pièce de résistance," said Sandra smugly.

"Thank god for that," Albert mumbled.

"Patricia the reverend's wife has been getting some very nasty hate mail lately, see exhibit A," Sandra said handing them several pieces of paper she found buried in the bottom of her handbag.

The letters were compiled in the usual village hate mail style of letters cut from Newspaper and Magazine article headings. Albert rolled his eyes, what a cliché. The first one read:

Roses are red
Violets are blue
I know and have proof of
What you've been up to!
What do you have to say about this Perfect Patricia?

And enclosed was a photograph of a young girl, probably in her twenties, posing nude. The girl was smiling but her eyes said something different.

"Needs to work on the old poetry skills," laughed Albert.

"That's Patricia when she was seventeen," said Sandra pointing at the photo. Apparently she made some money from posing like this when she was a girl. Her parents were terribly bad people by all accounts and she ran away from home, got in with a bad crowd and was desperate for cash. Her husband has no idea about her past and she is very keen that he doesn't find out about this."

The second one read:

Twinkle twinkle little star
I know exactly what you are
Babylonian whore I will reveal you to be
When you least expect it, just wait and see.
Don't you think Amelia is such a lovely name?

This one had a photograph of the reverend's wife talking to a man in what looked like park surroundings, the man's face was not visible but the discreet touch of their fingertips and eye contact was unmistakable.

"Who's Amelia?" asked Rose.

"She won't tell me, but I know she was extremely shook up over the mention of the name. Something else to do with her past perhaps. Either way she won't be pushed on the subject." Sandra shrugged.

"These are just two of them, there are loads more, some very serious indeed," said Sandra raising her eyebrows.

"Why hasn't she gone to the police then?" questioned Albert.

"She doesn't want a scandal. She's the vicar's wife after all. Mary said Patricia is very keen to know who is behind all this and try and deal with it as discreetly as possible rather than bring any shame and embarrassment on her husband. She's prepared to pay the going rate plus expenses"

After a long pause to allow Albert and Rose to take it all in Sandra asked excitedly, "Well? Are you in?"

Albert and Rose looked at each other and smiled.

"We're in," they said in unison and the squeal of delight that came out of Sandra was ear shattering.

"That's great news! I must let Mary know right away!" she said standing and gathering her things. "Keep hold of the letters for now bit of research and all that, I'll be in touch with the particulars, and remember, discretion is of the upmost importance!"

Chapter 2

Well it is true to say that there was nothing discreet about the ridiculous hat Rose wore that Sunday to Reverend Goodsoul's church. It was huge. Quite frankly something could have been nesting in it.

"Well I don't know what people wear to church these days!" said Rose when Albert nearly choked to death on his Weetabix when she appeared to breakfast this morning.

"We are supposed to be wearing our Sunday best, and this is the only hat I have so it will have to do."

"Well yes I understand that love but you bought this hat for that Caribbean cocktail fancy dress party!" laughed Albert. "It's got fake fruit and flowers on it and everything! Why don't you go the whole hog and put your coconut bikini on too!" Albert laughed even louder. They had been in too much of a rush for Rose to kill him immediately but she would certainly not forget to punish him later.

"Can't believe we are up this early on a Sunday," muttered Albert to Rose from the back pew as people were walking in to church. Rose was ignoring him, politely waving and nodding and saying "Good Morning" and smiling at complete random strangers.

"Didn't even finish my breakfast after you accidentally sent it flying this morning, so I'm starving," Rose continued to ignore him.

"Not to mention the fact that carrying your bags to the car this morning nearly completely done my back in," he continued to whisper. "What you got in there? A body or something?"

"I will have later if you don't shut up," Rose managed to reply through gritted teeth while still smiling and nodding at people. Albert sat quietly for a few moments, looking round with a mischievous face and wondering what he could do to placate his wife. He finally decided to pluck one of her own flowers out of her huge hat as subtly as possible before presenting her with it with a big cheesy grin.

"You are such a plonker," Rose couldn't help but smile. "Now behave. We are here to observe and learn and be nosy."

"So how will we recognise the wife with her clothes on?" Albert asked grinning as the reverend began his sermon.

After the service Albert and Rose loitered outside the church trying to spot Shirl's friend Denise's mum's sister Vera who works at the post office's twin brother George and wife Mary. It was a beautiful day in Upper Wobble. The Nutters hadn't yet had chance to explore the village having come straight from home but understood there was a room booked for them at The Mad Cow for as long as they needed it. The church was relatively small but beautiful. Stone walls, brown slate roof and one very large stained-glass window behind the altar.

The Nutters had been impressed with the reverend. He seemed like a kind gentle man, late forties at a guess and his belief in his words was admirable, contagious even Rose thought. He had brown, slightly greying short hair and was a tall slender man. His wife Patricia was currently stood by his side at the church entrance wishing the parishioners well, thanking them for coming and all that. She acted the part of vicar's wife well but you could tell her heart wasn't really in it.

Patricia was still as attractive as she had been in her youth, more so even. She had long wavy brown hair and hazel eyes and was just as tall and slender as her husband. Together they looked more like brother and sister than husband and wife. At that very moment, as Rose and Albert were staring at her, Patricia suddenly noticed them. She froze for a second then quickly tried to hide it. Whispered something in her husband's ear then began walking over to them.

At that moment Rose had a tap on the shoulder. "Ec ec eec excuse me are you Rose?" Rose turned round. George had the same bald patch and strange voice as his sister Vera, although he seemed to have a stammer as well as the bizarre whistling sound that appeared through his teeth, she could definitely see the family resemblance.

"You must be George," she said shaking his hand. "This is Albert, my husband," she said pointing to Albert who also shook George's hand smiling.

"An an and this is my wife Mary, Patricia's friend," George gestured to his wife. Mary was easily twenty years younger than George and quite an attractive lady. She had a bright floral dress on and bouncy blonde curls whereas George must have been late sixties, had about three hairs on his head and wore a long grey cardigan. They looked more like father and daughter than husband and wife. Patricia had arrived amongst the pleasantries.

"The Nutters I presume," she said shaking their hands, very abrupt and business-like. "My husband believes you to be friends of George and Mary here visiting the village for a few days so please play along and stick to that story wherever you go in the village. I do not want any gossip and speculation anywhere near my husband is that clear?" she said.

Albert felt like a naughty school boy. "Of course," said Rose smiling. "Discretion is our middle name," she said. At this Patricia looked up at Rose's ridiculously indiscreet hat and rolled her eyes.

"Follow me please," she said. "I have some tea prepared so we can talk properly in the vicarage. My husband will be working so won't be back for a while." Mary immediately followed Patricia, old George in pursuit as best he could with his stick and his limp and Rose and Albert followed slowly behind.

"Bit serious round here aren't they?" Albert muttered under his breath so only Rose could hear. "Feel like we'll get the cane if we are disobedient."

"You should be so lucky," whispered Rose.

Patricia led them into her lounge where she had tea cups and biscuits already prepared and on the coffee table. The cups were small and white with a few dainty flowers on them, exactly what you would expect from a vicar's wife. The lounge itself could not have been more obviously vicarage. Bright florals were everywhere, cushions, wallpaper, ornaments, photo frames, even the tea cosy! None of this seemed to have an ounce of Patricia's personality in it at all and I think Patricia knew exactly what they were thinking.

"I am my husband's second wife," she said while pouring tea. "His first wife Maud died rather tragically many years ago. It's a bit dated but the decor here is hers and my husband likes it this way," she said with a hint of sadness. "Please make yourselves comfortable," she said pointing to the fluffy floral sofa. George was already snoring in one of the arm chairs, Mary and Patricia sat down in unison on the other sofa opposite the Nutters.

After a short silence and a bit of uncomfortable tea slurping from Albert, Patricia said, "Can I please apologise for my abruptness. I promise you I'm not normally so sharp, it's just been a very difficult time for me lately with all this business. I'm not sleeping properly, constantly wondering what I have done that somebody is punishing me in this way. And to top it all off, this morning I received this." She left the room and quickly returned with a small brown envelope, she pulled out a photograph and handed it to Rose.

The photograph was in colour, sort of, yet weathered and showed an old tatty looking building, a large town house in fact. It was pretty dilapidated and tatty from the outside. Had a small front garden with an iron gate, overgrown plants and ivy, it was like something out of a horror film Albert thought.

"Does this place mean something to you?" said Rose. "Do you recognise it?" It was clear from her reaction that she did. Patricia took a deep breath.

"What I'm about to tell you I have never told anybody and it is not to leave these four walls," she said seriously. Albert and Rose shifted on the couch and leaned closer. Mary took her friend's hand. George continued to snore.

"I didn't have a happy childhood. My mother was an abusive drunk and my father I barely remember. I'm told he took his own life in when I was very young and I was ordered never to speak of him again. I was fifteen when I ran away. I stole some money from my mother, packed a bag, waited for her to fall asleep drunk in the armchair and left. I got on a bus and never looked back. I couldn't tell you now if my mother is alive or dead." She gave a small sad laugh at this and shook her head. "I did my best to forget that old life, although the few years that followed were not much better. You can probably guess how I lived from the photographs that you have already seen. I lived in a room in a house, that house," she said pointing to the photograph in Rose's hand. "I shared a room with three other girls, all trying to earn a living. Brothels were pretty commonplace in the eighties. The house was run by a horrid woman named Ida. She was a cold, hard faced woman. Took the money and the compliments from clients and gave us a roof over our head in return. I heard rumours of some even being sold, isn't that absurd!" she said. "I saw her you know, almost twenty years later. In my own hospital. She got cancer in the end. Died a slow painful death," she said quietly almost in a trance. "Some might call that justice." This woman had had an obviously bad effect on her life. "I had a friend there though, in that house, my first real friend. Her name was Amelia, which is why my heart sank when I got the poem,

Don't you think Amelia is such a lovely name?

I had been out one day, can't even remember where now and when I got home Amelia was gone. I was told she had decided to leave, packed her bags and went and we were to never ask questions or mention her name again. I knew something wasn't right. We had a pact you see, we were going to leave and start a fresh life away from the back streets of London. We were going to go to the sea, Cornwall or Devon and we had a plan and were putting tiny savings away in a tin hidden under a hole in the mattress. I know for a fact that she would not have left me as I wouldn't her, plus more importantly the money was still there in the tin, all of it. Surely she would have taken it if she had gone of her own free will, she would have needed it." You could hear the emotion in

Patricia's voice. This was obviously a difficult time in her life and she didn't want to talk about it.

"Do you mind me asking, Patricia, how you got out of there and how that girl became the vicar's wife?" asked Rose sensitively.

"Perhaps another time," she said having regained her composure and standing abruptly. "I feel I have probably already confessed too much." She began clearing the cups and noisily putting them back onto the tea tray; her hands were shaking.

"Nobody and I mean nobody knows about my past, who I was, where I lived, but whoever this is…" she trailed off shaking her head again. "Somehow whoever this is, they know and what's more they might even know what happened to Amelia. They know and are threatening to tell my husband what I was and ruin my life. And the worst part is they probably live here in this village, come to our church every Sunday, probably smile and shake my hand. I have no idea who it could be or how they found all this out. It would ruin my husband. He would be humiliated and disgusted with me." She wiped a tear from her eye.

"He might be more understanding than you think," said Mary kindly.

"No," said Patricia looking at the ground. "There are some sins that cannot be forgiven."

Once the Nutters had realised that they weren't going to get any more out of Trish, Mary walked the Nutters back to their car.

"I'm sorry if that was a bit intense," she said apologetically. "My friend has had a sad tragic life already and after finding stability and happiness finally someone wants to take that away from her, it's just madness. She is one of the happiest, funniest people I know and although her life may not be perfect she is happy in it. This person that she has become, this tired, frightened person is not her. She is a fighter. I do hope that you can help her."

"We will do everything we can to get to the bottom of this I promise you." Rose smiled kindly. Albert and Rose both knew that there was much more to this story than met the eye. Why was Patricia not telling them everything?

Mary began to walk back to the house. "Incidentally what is Patricia going to do with this person when we discover who it is?" Albert enquired.

She stopped and without even turning around said coldly, "You leave that to Trish."

Chapter 3

Poppy Nutter sailed through the busy pub delivering meals like a swan. She was a tall, long-legged, graceful girl, nothing at all like her mother. She was a happy smiley pretty thing, popular with all the customers, fantastic at her job and yet Felicity Bush hated her.

Her husband Nigel was a gibbering drooling wreck when she was around. It was embarrassing. Not to mention many of the regulars had the same reaction. Once, Felicity had accidentally on purpose tripped her up while she was carrying lunch to the old boys Bill and Jim, and rather than make a fuss (like they most definitely would have if Felicity had dropped their food) Bill and Jim were happy to get on their knees and eat their sandwiches and chips off the floor! Really quite ridiculous. Although Felicity knew that Poppy was only working her way through college so wouldn't be there forever, she wasn't sure she could cope with wiping her husband's slobber off the bar for much longer. Something had to be done.

*

The man sat in the corner of the pub, sipping his pint and pretending to read his book. He carefully and discreetly watched the tall, graceful, copper-haired waitress smiling and joking with some local men as she cleared their plates away. Something stirred in him. She reminded him of somebody, somebody from his past. Somebody whose similar beautiful smile had had to be wiped from her face. He would never forget that mocking smile. He told her then she would never laugh at him again and he was right. Now though, staring at this waitress those feelings of anger had come flooding back. Something had to be done.

*

"You can go on your break now, Poppy." Nigel the landlord said while smiling, breathing in and rubbing Poppy on the arm for rather longer than was necessary. "I've had the kitchen whip you up a sandwich."

"Oh thank you, Mr Bush, you are very kind. Is it vegetarian do you know because I was given a leaflet yesterday in the high street about how innocent animals are slaughtered unnecessarily and in awful ways in order to feed the human race – food they don't actually need as there is plenty of rice and vegetables to go around – and it shocked me. Do you know how they kill chickens? Well I couldn't believe how they killed chickens, hadn't really thought about it before but I just could not imagine eating chicken again after learning how they kill chickens, so have decided to be a vegetarian from now on."

"Well absolutely, I can completely see your point," Nigel said, listening intently to her every word. "You must tell me more about this, I'd be interested to see that leaflet." At that moment Felicity came out of the kitchen.

"Here is your sandwich," she said to Poppy almost dropping it onto the bar, a couple of crisps spilling off the side of the plate. "Back in twenty minutes to start getting organised for that big table coming in later, need to rearrange half the bloody pub for them by the looks of it."

"Felicity!" said Nigel "Is that a chicken sandwich?"

Felicity looked at Nigel like it was a trick question. What sat before them on the bar was quite clearly a chicken sandwich.

"How terribly insensitive of you! Poppy here is a vegetarian and would obviously not eat a chicken sandwich. What were you thinking? Do you know what they do to chickens before they become sandwiches?!" he said all flustered.

"What are you talking about? She had a ham sandwich yesterday!" Felicity raised her voice back at her husband.

"That's hardly the point, Felicity, don't be childish. We can't discriminate against things like this as employers," he said. "I'll get the kitchen to rustle you up something else, Poppy, cheese alright?" he said kindly.

"That would be great, Mr Bush, thank you so much for being so understanding. I'll be sat over by the window," she smiled and wandered off. Nigel beamed back at her then shook his head at his wife before heading off to the kitchen. Felicity just stood there confused. "What the hell just happened?" she thought to herself.

*

"Excuse me, sir?" the man in the corner of the pub had been so caught up in his own memories he hadn't even noticed the copper-haired waitress appear before him. She smiled at him, that beautiful mocking smile that he had tried so hard to forget.

"I'm ever so sorry but we need to rearrange this part of the pub for a private function this evening. Would you mind terribly if we asked you to sit over by the window perhaps? There's another beer in it for you if you go quietly," she laughed and winked at him.

"Not to worry," he said. "I was just getting ready to go anyway," he said standing up and closing his book and downing more than half a pint all at the same time.

"Oh," she said with what he thought sounded like disappointment in her voice.

"Don't worry I'll be back for that pint another time," he said to the girl. "You'll definitely be seeing me again." He smiled at her as he fumbled together his things and walked hurriedly towards the pub door. She noticed he was quite agile for a man with quite a profound limp.

*

Poppy didn't mean to frighten the man. He was definitely startled when she tapped his shoulder. He didn't look like a nervous man but he was certainly jumpy around her. He was quite a handsome man for his age, fifties perhaps. He had managed to make that one pint last for almost three hours and although they didn't need to start rearranging tables yet Felicity had ordered her to get rid of him seeing as he wasn't spending any money, hadn't even ordered any food.

As Poppy began wiping the table and collecting his empty glass, she noticed the man must have dropped his wallet; it was lying on the floor under the table. She grabbed it quickly and ran out the front door after him but he was nowhere to be seen. She was only seconds behind him. He certainly was quick for a man with a limp. It seemed like he must have vanished into thin air.

*

The man watched the copper-haired waitress as she came running out of the pub door and began searching for him. She wouldn't find him though. They never do. He had left his fake cards including his business card in the wallet and smiled to himself as he drove off and waited for her call.

Chapter 4

"Well, looks like this case is going to be a bit more interesting than gnome stealing and squished, I mean missing cats doesn't it?" Albert said to Rose as they drove away from the vicarage.

"I know," said Rose, "how on earth does someone go from being a you know what," Rose struggled with words like 'prostitute', her mother would have a heart attack if she heard such words come from her mouth "to being a Vicar's wife?"

"Oh they weren't kidding when they said the pub was just round the corner," laughed Albert. They had literally just put their seatbelts on when they arrived at their accommodation.

Turning the corner from the church they arrived at the centre of Upper Wobble. Ironically, Upper Wobble village was actually situated in a valley down a series of very steep hills. Here the main square of the town was extremely picturesque with a lovely green and water fountain in the middle. Shops and houses surrounded the square.

The Mad Cow was situated in the north east corner of the square. Several picnic benches were placed out the front on the patio which was nicely decorated like all pubs with hanging baskets and upside down flowerpots for ash trays. Rose immediately wanted to start being nosy or 'investigating' as she liked to call it but Albert insisted they check into The Mad Cow first so they could drop off their luggage and settle in before going for a wander.

Rose started towards the pub carrying her handbag, having a good look around while Albert struggled with the ridiculously oversized bags.

"Didn't realise we were staying 'til Christmas," Albert joked as he staggered along.

"For goodness sake Albert don't be silly, you'll put your back out," Rose said as Albert went to hand one of them to Rose. "You can pop back for the other one in a minute," she said wandering off empty handed.

"Thanks love, good idea," Albert said rolling his eyes. Rose smirked.

The Mad Cow's swinging pub sign could be seen from the car park and consisted of a cow's head with crossed eyes and tongue hanging out, rather funny the Nutters thought.

The inn had a small entrance way and a counter for the hotel on the right with a doorway behind it leading to somewhere or other, and a door into the main pub on the left and a large staircase leading up to the rooms.

The counter was unmanned at the moment but they could make out some hushed voices coming from behind the doorway and decided to wait patiently and listen in on the conversation rather than ring the bell after Rose shhhhhhed Albert.

"I told you it has to stop," whispered a male voice rather gruffly.

"And I told you what would happen if it did. Not only would I tell your wife about our little arrangement, I'll tell her about your other lady friend," retorted a female voice, certainly less whispered and discreet than the male voice. There was a short silence while the male voice took this new information in.

"How do you know about that?" said the man solemnly.

"You'd be surprised what I know," said the woman. "I suggest you keep up your end of the bargain or else I'll bring your whole world crashing down," said the woman with venom. With that a door slammed shut and there was silence.

After a few more moments of quiet, Rose felt it appropriate to ring the bell. A man appeared through the doorway looking a little dazed. He was a handsome man, in his forties perhaps, dressed in grey trousers and a rather creased white shirt, half tucked in. He nervously ruffled his hair as he approached the counter and seemed to finally pull himself together and with an extremely false smile approached the Nutters.

"How may I help you?" he said in quite a broad Scottish accent.

"We have a reservation," said Albert. "Name's Nutter".

"Of course," said the man scanning through his large red reservations book. "Here we are, double room for Mr and Mrs Nutter and our best suite too, overlooking the square. You should get a good view of the whole village from there," he said trying to sound jovial. "My name is Graham. The Mad Cow is run by me and my wife Denise who incidentally it was named after," he laughed rather falsely at his own joke. Albert and Rose both guffawed politely knowing full well this man had used that joke a million times before, probably his only joke in fact, looking at his serious red face.

"Anything you need just shout," said Graham handing them the key. Well, assuming the key was somehow attached to one end of the ridiculously huge green plastic key ring they were being handed.

"I'll get my boy to get your bags for you. Graham Junior!" he hollered towards the pub.

"Honestly we are fine with our bags," said Rose politely.

"Nonsense. Graham Junior!" he hollered once more nearly deafening the Nutters.

With that, a tall gangly-looking boy came strolling through the door. With bright ginger hair and a very pale complexion Graham Junior didn't look anything like his father. He had a very shy manner about him and seemed like one of those people that is frightened of everything.

"Take these bags up for our guests would you, Graham. Room 5, chop chop!" Young Graham began to gather up the Nutter's belongings with surprising strength and agility compared to the haphazard manner that Albert had carried them here.

Rose looked at Albert and gave him a look that said she knew he had been exaggerating when he was complaining about the weight of the bags and they followed gangly ginger Graham Jr up the stairs.

Well if this was The Mad Cow's best room the Nutters would hate to see their worst. Young Graham had gently put their bags down for them outside the door and gave them a polite nod before heading back down the stairs. After they had managed to manoeuvre the comedy size key/key ring into the lock and open the door, Albert had proceeded to fall face first into the room.

As with most old weird and wonderful pub inns there was a large step down into the room. I will not tell you what words followed from Albert's mouth. Rose stepped down the step and into the room gracefully behind him, stifling her giggles. The room was fairly small with one almost double bed in the middle. Albert and Rose knew that would be fun squeezing into later for two people of their size. There was just enough room for them to walk around the edge of the bed, sideways.

The quilt cover was white (ish) with some sort of flowery pattern on it. There was an old, dark, wooden wardrobe to the right of the door that looked like it might blow over if they opened the window. A chest of drawers sat at the end of the bed with ridiculously stiff drawers. Albert struggled to pull one open took one look at the ancient wallpaper lining in the bottom and then subsequently struggled even more to close it that he simply gave up. A TV sat on top of the chest of drawers that the Nutters thought should probably be in a museum and was almost certainly black and white. A little tiny kettle and cups and tea bags sat on a tray next to this. The curtains were old and had very thick green vertical stripes that went all the way to the floor. Albert dared not touch these for fear they might be moth infested. Although the room was small and looked like it had been transported here from the sixties, it was at least clean and fairly comfortable. It also had an extremely retro olive green bathroom suite, surprise surprise!

Old Graham on the desk though had been right about one thing, the view was amazing. From this window they could see all of the hustle and bustle of Upper Wobble. Handfuls of people with children and dogs were strolling through the park or eating picnics. There was a post office and newsagent near The Mad Cow, and a mini supermarket.

They could see high up a hill to the east was some sort of manor house. Rose made a mental note to enquire as to who lived there or if it was simply open to the public.

Other than the intriguing conversation the Nutters had overheard downstairs, Upper Wobble seemed like a pleasant fairly idyllic place. Couldn't possibly contain the scandals and affairs of the reverend's wife or could it...?

Chapter 5

After fighting with the stiff chest of drawers and being particularly delicate to the wardrobe that looked like it would give way to woodworm and disintegrate at any moment, Rose and Albert decided to take a stroll round the village of Upper Wobble. It had also occurred to them to get something light for lunch while they were out as they had already decided to try The Mad Cow's food that evening along with half the wine list.

There was no sign of either Graham as the Nutters went out the front door of the inn into the sunshine. It was a truly glorious day in the village of Upper Wobble. The Nutters couldn't believe they had lived less than thirty minutes away from this village and never visited. Rose stopped to admire some postcards on a stand outside of the newsagents while Albert's nose and hungry stomach led him towards a nearby pie stall.

"Two pounds a pie or three for a fiver," said the woman on the stall to Albert rather encouragingly. Albert would have guessed she was mid-forties, well presented, and was wearing a floral dress and a pinny. "All homemade, by little old me, Upper Wobble's finest," she said giving Albert a beaming smile. "You look like a steak and ale pie man to me," she said as she began putting three pies in a paper bag. "I'll bag you some up shall I?" she said having already bagged them up and thrusting them toward Albert's hands before he could answer.

"I wouldn't eat those if I were you," said a rather sarcastic voice over Albert's shoulder. He turned to see a very attractive lady, also he would guess in her forties. She had curly blonde hair, bright red lipstick and remarkably white teeth. The woman linked her arm through Albert's and whispered rather loudly and not remotely discreetly in Albert's ear.

"Rumour has it that Penny here is responsible for the deteriorating cat population in Upper Wobble if you know what I mean," she smirked.

"Well rumour also has it that Denise here is responsible for the Upper Wobble chlamydia outbreak," retorted Penny still holding onto the bag of pies. The two women glared at each other for a moment, Denise – the lady with the lipstick – now holding Albert's arm rather more tightly. There was no way Albert was running away from this uncomfortable situation anytime soon. The two women continued to glare at each other. Albert gulped.

"Thought I'd find you near the pies," said a familiar voice from behind. Albert could not remember the last time he had been this happy to see Rose. Rose was eying the lipstick lady suspiciously who, catching Rose's evil eye, released Albert's arm.

"I'm Denise, landlady of The Mad Cow," she beamed at Rose extending her hand for Rose to shake it. Penny rolled her eyes and went back to her pies. Albert, knowing his wife's ridiculously strong 'I don't like you' handshake could put the toughest of men on their knees, decided to intervene and shook Denise's hand.

"I'm Albert and this is my wife Rose. We are just visiting the village for the weekend, coincidentally staying at The Mad Cow," Albert gushed.

"Oh you are the Nutters. Excellent, excellent. I assume you have already had the pleasure of my husband," she said trying to stifle a hint of venom with a bittersweet smile.

"Anyway must dash, so much to do. See you both later then!" and with that she rushed off into the market crowd and was gone.

Rose turned to give Albert her best "Well?" look.

"What?!" he smiled.

"Sir would you like the pies?" Penny the pie lady said rather cautiously.

"Yes please," Rose interjected. "They smell delicious," she said getting her purse out.

"I apologise for that little charade. Denise and I haven't seen eye to eye for a long time," she smiled apologetically.

"Well with friends like that who needs enemies?" Albert joked.

"Oh she's not my friend," Penny gave a small bitter laugh. "She's my sister."

Rose and Albert sat on a bench eating Penny's pies, watching the village go by.

"Well if this is cat, it's my new favourite meat," Albert joked. Rose had to agree. Despite Denise's scathing remarks towards her sister's pies they were quite possibly the best the Nutters had ever tasted and Albert knew his stuff where pies were concerned.

"Wonder what could have happened in their past to make two sisters hate each other like that?" Rose asked aloud.

"Probably over some bloke," Albert said. "You know what women are like," he said innocently, clearly forgetting who he was sat with. "Reckon that Denise would tell you anything after a few vinos that one," he chuckled. "See what Graham meant now when he said The Mad Cow was named after his wife." The Nutters both laughed at this. "Anyway it's none of our business and nothing to do with our case. I can see you thinking about it, nosy," Albert laughed.

"I'm not nosy!" exclaimed Rose. "I'm inquisitive," she said in her defence. "Plus how do you know it's nothing to do with what's happening to the vicar's wife? She's being sent hate mail and being called a 'Babylonian whore' and that is most definitely the work of a woman."

*

Mary and George were already sat at a table in The Mad Cow when Rose and Albert came down for dinner. Mary had called and arranged to have dinner with the Nutters so she could fill them in on any relevant or irrelevant local gossip and give them a rundown of who's who in the village.

Mary looked particularly glamorous, Rose got the impression she was one of those women who got out of bed looking glamorous. Her yellow curly hair had a pretty white flower clipped into it. She was wearing another flowery dress, this one dark blue and much more hugging than the one she wore to church. George, still looking like he could be her father, wearing a lovely beige diamond-patterned cardigan spotted them first and waved them over. The Nutters exchanged pleasantries and joined them at the table.

"Let me get some drinks in," Albert said. "Usual love?" he said to Rose who smiled and nodded appreciatively. George and Mary ordered a glass of white and a glass of red wine respectively.

Albert returned with their drinks wobbling and clinking on a tray, manoeuvring his way round other tables, trying not to elbow people in the head. Turns out Albert and Rose's usual when eating out was a bottle of red for Albert and a bottle of white for Rose.

"That should keep us going until dinner arrives," Albert joked. George and Mary looked on a little disapprovingly but smiled politely. Albert and Rose exchanged a look that meant clearly these two aren't party animals, so must behave.

The foursome began the usual chitchat amongst couples meeting for the first time while browsing the menu when Denise turned up to take their order. It was clear that Denise had been sampling her own bar (a regular occurrence, Mary pointed out).

"Nutters!" she exclaimed, with a slight wobble on her approach. "Hope everything is to your liking in your room, everything comfortable?" Before they could reply there was a loud clang from behind the bar.

"Graham Junior! For heaven's sake!" Graham's ginger head popped over the top of the bar; his face had gone bright red. He appeared to have slipped or tripped as he scrambled to his feet and emerged carrying several trays.

"Honestly that boy will give me a heart attack one day. Never known anyone so useless. Just like his father," she said scathingly, then seeing the serious faces at the table in front of her she followed this by a very over the top high pitched laugh to indicate that it was clearly a joke. The Nutters weren't so sure.

Denise staggered off to the kitchen once she had taken their orders, leaning over the bar to grab her drink hidden underneath and have a good slurp.

"Do do don't worry she doesn't cook it," George said with his gentle stammer, and laughing on seeing their worried faces "Denise always has a few on Su Su Sundays. Well and the other days of the week too," he laughed again. Rose thought him quite a nice jolly old chap when he was awake.

"Chitchat over," said Mary seriously. "Let me give you the goss on the local yokels" she smiled rather slyly at this. Clearly one who thrived on gossip.

"Let's start with The Mad Cow herself shall we," she said quietly nodding towards Denise who now sat at the end of the bar propped on a bar stool, glass in hand, flicking through a magazine. "As you can see she drinks like a fish and has ended up in one or two awkward situations as a result."

"Ooh ooh like the time she was found on the bench in the square asleep with lipstick smudged all over face and her blouse undone," George added excitedly.

"Yes quite. She claimed she'd felt unwell and unbuttoned her blouse as she was having a hot flush and must have passed out," Mary said raising her eyebrows.

"Oh oh and there was the time at Mr Ponsonby-Gables' annual summer bash where she stepped outside to get some fresh air, came back an hour later wearing no bra! Now normally I'm too much of a gentleman to notice these things but she went straight on to the dance floor, dress half tucked into her knickers, dancing away, white linen see through dress and strobe lights, bad combination," he shook his head disapprovingly.

"I'm sorry I missed that," joked Albert. Rose kicked him under the table.

"Ooh and then there was the time…"

"Yes thank you George," Mary interrupted. "I think they get the idea." George was quiet at once. Obviously got told off quite a lot. Mary was not the sort of woman who could be argued with. His stammer seemed to improve however when he was excited the Nutters noticed.

"That poor orange-haired son of hers can never do anything right, same as her husband." They could see grown up Graham through the door looking at some paperwork behind the desk where they had checked in earlier. "He plays the sweet doting husband and she does nothing but criticise them, neither Graham ever stands up to her." Graham came into the pub carrying the paperwork and leant in to kiss his wife on the cheek. Denise turned away and carried on reading her magazine without even acknowledging him. The Nutters felt rather sorry for him at that point although they both still remembered the heated conversation they had overheard while checking in. Doting Graham also had a secret, one that he was being blackmailed for by an unknown woman. Perhaps the same woman sending hate mail to the Vicar's wife. Maybe Denise already knows and that is why she is so cold towards him, Rose mused.

"Speaking of Mr Ponsonby-Gables," Mary whispered, "that is him over there with those giggling women." The Nutters had noticed the well-dressed middle aged man sat with one arm around two girls who were perhaps early twenties. The three of them had clearly had lots to drink and were giggling and laughing loudly at their own jokes.

"He's wealthy, owns that big house on the hill, thinks as he's rich he owns the place. Has a big summer and Christmas bash and invites half the village and get this." She leaned in closer and lowered her voice. "Trish told me once that he tried it on with her at one of these bashes, had one too many gin and tonics and cornered her in the kitchen getting ice cubes while everyone else was outside on the lawn. She was quite frightened, she said, he started to get quite physical and would not take no for an answer. It was only the fact that Denise stumbled in having taken a wrong turn on her way to the loo that he let her go and she was able to get away. She soon made her excuses and her and the vicar left pretty early. She's pretty tough though, wouldn't tell her husband, blamed the alcohol but I reckon Gables would pull that trick sober. Nobody really likes him to be honest, he's an arrogant irksome little man."

"We all go for the free booze and food," George smiled. Albert nodded approvingly, his sort of party. "Ooh next weekend is his summer bash, I wonder if we could get you an invite, be a great place to meet and greet the village properly, be perfect mingling excuse for the case at hand, wouldn't it Mary?" he looked to his wife.

"Oh I don't think the Nutters would want to go to that," Mary seemed to stumble on her words. "I'm sure they will have much better things to do for the investigation."

"Nonsense!" said George. "How better to see the community all as one, let them know we aren't all bad." George laughed, The Nutters smiled politely, Mary forced a smile.

How strange that she had seemed so helpful before but for some reason she didn't want the Nutters attending Mr Ponsonby Whats-his-face's party thought Rose. Invite or not, free booze and food Albert was already going she knew and smiled to herself.

The table remained silent for a time, thankfully this was broken by the arrival of dinner. Rose's nearly landed in her lap as it was not so delicately placed on the table by the continuously drinking Denise, several potatoes had in fact jumped off her plate as it landed at a rather lopsided angle.

Albert received more of Denise's cleavage in his face than food when she placed his on the table. George must have known to wear his lovely patterned cardigan as it hid the gravy splashes quite well that continued to appear much to the annoyance of his wife. It was obviously a regular occurrence. Mary barely touched hers and seemed to push it round the plate. She had definitely lost her appetite. The Nutters both cleared their plates, Albert would have (if at home) licked the plate, but after seeing his wife's evil stare at him he thought better of it.

George having moved onto brandies after dinner could be seen gradually getting sleepier and sleepier until he was in fact asleep. Again. Strangely Mary wasn't embarrassed by all of

George's falling asleep habits but she seemed to relax once he was snoring.

"So who are the two women with Mr Ponsonby-Gables?" Rose enquired after a short silence hoping to get Mary back to gossip.

"Well," she smiled and seemed glad of the distraction. "That is Tracy and Michelle. They own the hair and beauty salon down the road. Larger than life loud characters obviously, no idea why they are here in a quiet little village when they should in my opinion be anywhere else," she said a little scathingly. Seeing their surprised reaction she added, "Oh don't get me wrong, they are nice enough girls but they are so loud and really quite vulgar for young ladies. Have had one or two run ins with Patricia over it too. Being an upstanding member of the community she has pulled them up over their inappropriate behaviour a number of times, often publicly."

"Has she embarrassed them enough for them to send her hate mail do you think?" Albert asked, Rose was thinking the same thing.

"God no!" Mary laughed "They haven't got enough brain cells between them to pull this off," she continued to laugh and shake her head. The Nutters would later, on meeting Tracy and Michelle (or Trace and 'Chelle as they were more commonly known) understand Mary's laughter at this point.

"Anyway, I'm going to get this one home," she said nodding towards sleepy George. There was a slight sad sigh that followed. The age difference between them must put some strain on the marriage thought Rose. She was desperate to learn how their relationship had come to be.

"Your dinner is on expenses, please order dessert if you wish," she said kindly as she gently nudged and woke up her husband. "We'll catch up tomorrow no doubt," she said leading George towards the door.

"I could get used to this," Albert said already browsing the dessert menu with a huge smile on his face when Mary suddenly stopped and turned and walked back to them.

"Please do your best to help my friend. Trish hasn't been the same since all this business started. The fire in her seems to have died. She's frightened, and distant and I miss her terribly," she said sadly. "I will do absolutely whatever it takes to get her back. I thought I'd never be able to repay Trish for what she has done for me but solving this might go some way towards that. I owe her so much. She saved my life once and now I must save hers. Please let me know if there is anything you need." With that she left.

Albert and Rose's heads were spinning with a million questions. How had Patricia the vicar's wife saved her friend's life? How many people in this village had a grudge against her? Just how badly could she have humiliated Tracy and Michelle the salon party girls? Would Mr Ponsonby-Gables take revenge on her spurning his advances? How did a teenage runaway stripper even become a vicar's wife? Who had been threatening to expose Graham's secrets in the back room behind The Mad Cow's check in desk? What had happened between Denise and her pie making sister Penny to make them despise each other so? And more importantly how on earth was Denise still sat upright on that bar stool?

Chapter 6

"Oy Ramsbottoms, drink up!" Felicity shouted towards Dave and Sandra who sat at the bar of The Wobble Inn like they did most Sunday evenings. "We closed ages ago," she said having a good slurp of her vodka and hint of lemonade, just how Felicity liked it. Poppy Nutter smiled and continued to wipe down the tables. Everyone had left except for Uncle Dave and Auntie Sandra; they all called them that as they had been friends of her parent's for as long as Poppy could remember.

"Oh one for the road, eh?" Dave said nudging his wife playfully who in turn giggled.

"We've all got homes to go to you know," Felicity said turning off lights, vodka still in hand, slight wobble.

"Come on, you've only got to go upstairs," laughed Dave. "Go on, one more for me and Sand and one for yourself, make it a double," he said playfully, knowing full well this worked every time. Felicity's mood changed instantly when someone offered to buy her a drink, especially a double.

"Oh Dave you are kind," she said smiling. "Go on then just one more, help me sleep tonight," she said, already pouring the vodka and toasting him in her usual way. "All the breast!" they both laughed.

Poppy laughed. This little routine went on nearly every Sunday evening except that normally her parents were here too having drinks with the Ramsbottoms. She wondered how they were getting on in the village of Upper Wobble on their first real case. She was very proud of them indeed, well as long as they solved it that is. She knew how much her father hated having to leave the police force through injury, it had broken his heart. Since starting this private investigator business though a new lease of life had been released. Her daddy was getting back to his old self. Perhaps now he was busier he would pay less attention to the boys in her life she thought. He was extremely overprotective having known through experience the very worst of human kind but setting Allan on whoever dared knock the door for her was one step too far. Allan seemed to share his master's views on 'boys' as he very rarely moved except for when an unsuspecting suitor knocked the door to take Poppy on a date.

"Nigel me old chap," Dave said as he spotted Nigel returning to the bar with glasses he had collected outside. "What you having? One for the road." Felicity began pouring her husband's pint knowing exactly what he would have. "What about you Pops?" he said swivelling round on the bar stool.

"No thanks Uncle Dave. Got college in the morning, I'll be heading off soon."

"Boooooooooo," Dave, Sandra and Nigel said in unison, and all laughed, usual banter for someone who refused a drink in The Wobble Inn. Felicity didn't boo, she quietly cheered.

"Go on get off early love," Nigel said putting one arm round Poppy. "You've worked extremely hard today." Felicity rolled her eyes. More work for me to do, she thought to herself.

"Oh well if you are sure, Mr Bush, that's terribly kind of you," she said smiling sweetly.

Poppy went to gather her coat and bag, before giving Uncle Dave and Auntie Sandra a quick peck on the cheek. It was then that she noticed the wallet on the back of the bar that the man with the limp had dropped earlier.

"Oh damn. Completely forgot to call that man who had dropped his wallet," she said.

"Well he won't appreciate you calling him at this hour about it," Felicity said. "I'll get Nigel to call him in the morning," she said, practically pushing Poppy out the door. "Hurry up then girl, want to lock up." Poppy said her goodbyes and stood on the outside doorstep buttoning up her coat. It had grown surprisingly chilly after such a beautiful day and all was quiet in the village of Little Wobble. She heard the door being bolted behind her. God only knows what time Dave and Sandra would leave, she smiled to herself. Depends how many vodkas they buy Mrs Bush.

She slung her handbag onto one shoulder, put her hands in her pockets and began the small walk home, through the quiet deserted village. She had done this walk a million times but tonight she felt a little uncomfortable and quickened her pace.

*

The man watched the copper-haired waitress. Standing where he knew he wouldn't be seen. He watched her with awe. She so looked like somebody he used to know it made him smile.

He had been angry at first that she hadn't called him about his lost wallet but then it occurred to him that she may be playing hard to get, or even that she was waiting for him to come back in the pub and get it from her personally. But he couldn't wait that long. He had to see her now. Had to touch that copper hair, to smell her skin. He hoped she would smell like the woman in his memories. The thought aroused him. He had to focus though, he had to concentrate.

He watched her walk under the glow of the streetlight turning the corner out of sight. He pulled up his collar against the slight chill, stepped out of his hiding place and began to follow her.

*

Poppy always felt safe walking home. Nothing bad ever happened in their village. Besides it was such a short walk, sometimes her brother or dad would come meet her taking Allan for a late evening walk (much to Allan's disgust) or whatever boy she was seeing at the time would meet her and walk her home. Not all the way to the front door of course because her dad and Allan could sniff out a teenage boy's testosterone a mile off. Tonight for some reason though she felt a little uneasy.

She kept looking over her shoulder thinking she could hear footsteps nearby but there was nothing there. It was chilly tonight and she wanted to get home quickly so she decided she would take the short cut down the alleyway that ran behind the gardens of Maple Street and came straight out into her road, Little Wobble Lane. The alley was dark and lit simply by a street lamp at the far end. She hurried on, then a shadow appeared at the end of the alley in front of her, the shadow of a man, a man with a dog. The dog immediately ran towards her and lunged.

*

"Allan you nutter!" she said to the dog as he placed his huge paws on her shoulders and began licking her face. Her younger brother Charlie had decided to bring Allan for walkies to escort her home.

"You scared me to death," she said putting one arm around Charlie's neck and rustling his already messy hair.

"Sorry Pops," he smiled. "Couldn't keep hold of Allan's lead, bloody mutt. I was home alone bored and Allan hasn't been out today so thought we'd come meet you didn't we boy?" he said rubbing Allan's cheeks playfully and collecting the end of his lead.

"Well I'm very glad you did," Poppy said. "I'll make the bacon sarnies when we get in, I'm starving."

"Thought you were veggie now?" Charlie laughed and tripped over a slightly raised paving stone at the same time.

"Nah, decided it wasn't for me. A vegetarian Nutter, dad would never hear of it," she laughed.

*

The man watched the copper-haired waitress leave the alley way with the boy and the dog. They weren't part of the plan. The boy he could have dealt with but the dog. He shuddered at the memories. He had a terrible fear of dogs since his childhood. This was going to be more difficult than he thought, something would have to be done about the dog for him to get near to her. He watched them open a gate to the front garden of a particularly well looked after front garden at that. He could hear them chatting and laughing as they walked into the front door of number 42 Little Wobble Lane. "Tonight is not the night my love," he thought to himself. "But I now know where you live," he smirked to himself as he turned back towards the alleyway and back to his car.

Chapter 7

The Nutters awoke to another beautiful day in the village of Upper Wobble. They hadn't had the best night's sleep due to the fact that the bed was narrower than the Nutters were side by side so they had been forced to 'spoon' all night. Albert awoke with the worst case of pins and needles in his arm he had ever experienced where Rose had been laid on it all night. A similar pain was forming in his brain for he and Rose had decided to sample one or two more drinkies before finally being asked by Graham politely to go to bed (Denise had been escorted to bed an hour previous by her husband after she fell asleep in the loo).

Albert had also felt quite a chill last night. Despite the sunny day there was a definite temperature drop during the night, not that Rose would have noticed having been wrapped up in ninety per cent of the duvet all night. On top of that The Mad Cow's sign which was just outside their window had swung and creaked as loudly as it possibly could all night. To summarise, Albert was going to be tired and cranky today.

He tried to discreetly slide his arm out from under Rose's head without waking her, however she stirred as soon as he moved.

"What a lovely sleep," she said sleepily smiling. He looked at her in disbelief and shook his head. "Put the kettle on love," she said stretching, hugely doing starfish impressions on the bed pushing him out.

"Yes dear. Already doing it," he filled the kettle from the tap in the bathroom and flicked the switch. As the kettle began to whistle he opened the curtains and stood looking upon the village of Upper Wobble once more. Rose got out of bed and stood beside him. Yawning, she rested her head on his shoulder.

Although it couldn't have been later than half seven in the morning they appeared to be the last people in the village to get out of bed. Once again the village was full of people bustling about. There were children in school uniforms stood outside the newsagents already eating sweets. Mums with pushchairs, lads on bikes, old ladies with trollies queuing outside the post office. They noticed Tracy and Michelle jogging together in Lycra leggings and tops, still constantly nattering. A few stalls were setting up again; Denise's sister Penny and her pies being one of them. Rose noted a stall further down that sold handbags which she hadn't noticed yesterday, would definitely be investigating that later she thought to herself. As if knowing what she was thinking Albert turned to her

"You've got enough bloody handbags," they both laughed.

They decided to hit the ground running today. Albert was first to try the shower, unsurprisingly one of those that flashed between hot and freezing cold resulting in screams coming from Albert more high pitched, Rose thought, than the time on the way home from The Wobble Inn Dave had dared him to try and vault over a concrete bollard.

Rose, rooting through her handbag, decided to catch up on a quick Dear Doris letter before they attacked the pub fry up breakfast downstairs. It took her ages to find anything in this handbag; she definitely needed another, she chuckled to herself as she finally produced a little wad of letters that the Daily Wobble newspaper had posted to her. She had five envelopes all addressed to Doris. Normally an agony aunt would try to read all of her correspondence and then reply in the order of the most serious letter to the person that needed the advice more *urgently.* As it was she wouldn't have time so she laid the envelopes out on the desk, mixed them all up, shut her eyes and picked one.

Dear Doris

My son recently brought home a girl to meet me (his doting mother) for the first time and I don't like her at all. She

is at least fifteen years younger than him for starters, has appalling table manners, laughs with her mouth full. Told me my late husband was very handsome while looking at one of my photographs (to which I pointed out that it was actually me in that photo not my husband.) Just plain rude. She even broke one of my favourite mugs trying to wash up after I made them tea!

My son has never needed another woman in his life before now, just his mother and now he is even talking about moving in with her. He is 50 this year and I wanted to take him to the seaside at Skegness like we used to when he was a boy as a surprise but she has already planned a holiday abroad somewhere warm and sunny for him! The sheer cheek of it!

I am in need of some advice, Doris. This woman is no good for him I can sense it like only a mother can. Please help.

Worried, Enid, 72, Wobble on the Marsh

Rose sighed. Just once she would love a juicy letter. Preferably something out of a soap opera. What she wouldn't give for a "Dear Doris, I'm pregnant and the father could be any one of Wobble FC" or "Dear Doris, I've taken to wearing my wife's knickers".

Dear Enid

I am sorry to hear that you are in distress. As a parent we all from time to time will not look favourably upon our children's partners. My husband has been known to set the dog on my daughter's more than once. As is usually the case in these situations, making these feelings you have known to your son will only make him dislike and resent you and push him further towards this woman.

I had sympathy when you said she was fifteen years younger than him imagining a spotty teenager or something, right up until the point you told me he was 50! I think you know deep down Enid that a man age 50 still living with his mum in the first place is a tad unusual.

With regards to your son's new girlfriend, I'm sure it is much harder for her to meet you and live up to your standards (which are obviously very high). Breaking your mug while washing up! I wish some of the girls my eldest brings home knew where the sink was! Not to mention I think we would all pick a sunny holiday abroad over Skegness given the chance wouldn't we.

If you are honest with yourself I bet you haven't seen your son this happy in a long time.

People don't like change but things can often change for the better. I understand this will be hard for you but we must all let our children fly the nest even if it breaks our hearts (I keep pushing mine but they just won't go!). Keeping him prisoner will only make him resent you. Do the kind thing and give your son and his new lady your blessing with the promise that you will be there should things go wrong like all us mothers are. He will love and value you even more, and who knows he might in return bless you with grandchildren.

Your friend, Doris

She sealed the envelope, making a mental note to visit the post office for some stamps later before heading off to breakfast with her husband, who was about to pass out he was so hungry apparently.

Considering the amount of alcohol she had consumed the previous evening, Denise was bright eyed and bushy tailed, all smiles and chats as she brought them their breakfast.

"Morning!" she shrieked at them rather too loudly for Albert's headache. "How did you sleep?" she asked. "Perfectly well I'm sure in our best room. We have been praised on our comfort levels before," she said, rather satisfied with herself, before they could answer.

"We slept wonderfully didn't we Albert?"

"Wonderful," Albert lied politely. A huge clang seemed to emanate from the kitchen at that point, startling them all.

"That boy will be the death of me," Denise said clutching her chest. "Excuse me a moment," she said oh-so-politely and smiling.

The Nutters watched her storm into the kitchen and could overhear various raised voices from within. Graham Junior suddenly appeared covered from his head in, from where the Nutters sat, what looked like blood. Denise appeared shortly after.

"Now what can I get you? We have everything except plum tomatoes I'm afraid. Appear to have run out."

The Nutters were once again extremely impressed with the quality of the food from The Mad Cow. After a huge breakfast and three coffees Albert's headache had subsided and he was ready and raring to go.

They decided to divide and conquer for the first part of their day, exploring the village, having various bits of chit chat with complete strangers, trying to piece together some clues, and then meet in the park area on the same bench they had munched one of Penny's pies yesterday armed with more pies, and compare notes. Patricia was unavailable today but had invited them for lunch tomorrow for an update on progress. Hopefully they would have something to tell her.

Rose took off for the post office to get her stamps and start gossiping while Albert went back to the room to collect his wallet. He was just coming down the stairs heading towards the front door when he overheard Graham in the back room behind the check in desk. This time he was on the phone and talking very discreetly. Albert stopped before he reached the last step and tried to listen as best he could.

"I don't think I can get away today," he said then waited for the response. "I know I said I would but I just can't, it's manic here, plus Denise is out all afternoon, God knows where this time, and I'm here on my own. I'm sorry." Again silence while the caller replied. "Tomorrow definitely, at the usual place." Response. "Yes I'm looking forward to it too. See you then." He put the phone down and came out from the back room, looking startled to see Albert.

"Mr Nutter, how are you today? Did you sleep well? How was breakfast?" he said trying to sound casual.

"Everything is great thank you, really enjoying The Mad Cow," he said smiling. He made a mental note to find out exactly who Graham was meeting tomorrow and why as he pushed the pub doors open onto the glorious morning sunshine in Upper Wobble.

Rose joined the queue of old ladies at the post office. Normally she would be looking at her watch, impatient to get moving but not today. She was soaking up the atmosphere and eavesdropping on conversations. You couldn't beat village life for gossip and backstabbing.

She saw George behind the counter, his usual smiling self. Today he was sporting a chunky maroon knitted cardigan and spectacles on the end of his nose. He was a lovely smiley chap but she still couldn't quite figure out how his marriage to Mary had happened. She wondered if she might get the chance to ask Patricia tomorrow afternoon.

As the queue moved on just in front of her there was a bespectacled woman at the counter, probably about forty with thick glasses and dark hair stretched back across her head into a tight bun. She had a long skirt, flat shoes and one of those long thick cardigans that covers your bum.

"So ss s sorry to hear about your mum Joyce," George was saying kindly. "I heard she has taken a turn for the worse."

"Thank you George," she said with a sigh.

"If there is anything I can do. Although it might be time to get proper help Joyce, give yourself a break," he said sympathetically.

"Why does everyone keep saying that?" she said rather loudly this time. "I can cope perfectly well, I am coping perfectly well," she said sharply as if trying to reassure herself.

"I didn't mean to offend, Joyce, there is no doubt that you are coping but surely you are entitled to help too," he tried.

"My mother would rather die than go into a home where horrible strangers poke and prod and feed and wash you. Look at her dear friend Maud, she went in and never came out." The name Maud struck a bell in Rose's head. Could this woman be referring to Maud, the vicar's first wife? She would have to find out. "I wish people would just stop poking their noses into our business," Joyce said and gathered her things and stormed out of the post office before George could reply. Rose approached the counter with a smile.

"Morning George."

"M M Morning Rose," he said sighing. "Poor girl," he said nodding towards the door where Joyce had just left. "Looks after her mother all by herself, she's very sick, physically and mentally. It's too much for her really but she won't get help. Bit of a battleaxe her mother mind you. Never would let her daughter have much of a life even as a youngster."

"That's sad," said Rose genuinely. "I couldn't help but overhear her mention Maud," she said, "Is it the same…" George interrupted before she could finish.

"The vicar's first wife Maud, yes. She was taken very ill, very young and died in a care home. So sad," Before Rose could ask any more questions he said, "Goodness me look at the queue, here we are waffling! What can I get you Rose?" A large queue had indeed emerged behind Rose; she had been so engrossed she hadn't even noticed. Her questions would have to wait until later. She purchased her stamps and headed back outside into the square.

Albert Nutter decided to take a slow and steady stroll to the newsagent's. There he could buy a couple of newspapers – both national – for the real world news and the local Daily Wobble for all news in the Wobble regions. He could also purchase his favourite bar of chocolate and hope Rose didn't catch him eating it. He had had to cut back recently on all things sweet after finding out he was diabetic. Only tablet-controlled at the moment, nothing too serious but Rose was not allowing him to take any chances.

After George and Mary had left last night she had snatched the dessert menu out of his hands and bonked him on the head with it. She did however let him have another brandy instead so that went some way to making up for it.

Albert browsed the postcard stand outside grabbing an amusing calendar girls style saucy village humour postcard for Dave on the way. He wandered into the newsagent's and browsed the newspaper and magazine section. The usual tabloids splashed with big red text, a few ladies magazines. 'Stop! Eavesdrop', 'Rumours & Bloomers' and 'OMG! Did you see…?' he noticed, Poppy's favourites. He collected his papers off the shelf before wandering off to the sweet section.

He paid the old lady behind the counter and headed out the door already browsing his newspaper when he managed to walk into someone who in turn dropped their shopping bag on the floor.

"God I'm so sorry he said to the man," as they both began gathering the items off the floor. "Christ I can be clumsy at times!" he exclaimed as they both stood up together.

"That's no problem," said the vicar smiling, "accidents happen." Albert went bright red. Not only had he sent the vicar and his shopping flying after being told to be discreet and subtle and not attract too much attention, he had also managed to say both God and Christ in his opening sentences to the man!

"Oh you dropped this," the vicar said, bending down to pick up the saucy postcard of half-naked village ladies with Belgian buns and cups of tea covering their bits. Albert wanted the floor to swallow him whole. Rose would be in hysterics when he told her about this later.

"Thank you father," he said blushing. "S'for a friend," he said waving the postcard about, "and apologies again." He stuffed the post card inside one of the papers.

"It's Mr Nutter isn't it?" the vicar said as Albert started to walk away. "Friend of George and Mary's?" he eyed Albert suspiciously.

"Yes," he said. "Oh and you must be their friend the vicar," he said rather stupidly. "Reverend Goodsoul."

"Yes, please call me Peter," he smiled kindly, extending his hand for Albert to shake. "George and Mary said you were visiting. It's very nice to meet you." He put his shopping down so he could shake Albert's hand with both hands in the genuine vigorous manner of a man who really means it. "Any friends of theirs are friends of ours. Please you must come to dinner, my wife Patricia is a fantastic cook. I'll invite George and Mary too obviously. Shall we say this evening?"

"Well yes that would be lovely thank you, Reverend," Albert said genuinely. So far they seemed to have done nothing but eat while being in Upper Wobble, not that Albert minded at all but Rose would be watching his every move and not allowing him any desserts. Still he had his sneaky chocolate bar that he had just purchased which he would now enjoy without her knowing (he hoped).

After exchanging a few more pleasantries with the reverend they went their separate ways. Albert noticed a small café on the other side of the square which he thought would be the perfect place to firstly, get a nice cup of tea, secondly, munch on his naughty choccie bar, thirdly, to read his papers, fourthly, to write out Dave's postcard, and fifthly, to make some notes on all the key points, events and discussions that they had learned so far.

As Albert walked in through the door of 'Upper Wobble Buns' he was surprised to notice Mary behind the counter.

"Morning Albert," she said kindly but very tiredly. "Did you sleep well?" Why does everyone keep asking that? he thought to himself. "Take a seat and I'll bring you a cuppa," she said indicating a table in the window.

"I didn't know you worked here," Albert said smiling at Mary.

"Actually I own it," she said. "I always dreamt as a little girl of running my very own café. I always pictured it somewhere near the seaside, full of tourists and local little old ladies," she said almost dreamily. "Upper Wobble obviously has no seaside but its close enough to the dream. George brought it for me a couple of years ago. The best present I've ever had." She smiled a melancholic smile. For all the age gap between Mary and George she was certainly very fond of him and the affection could be heard in her voice. Still would be fascinated to know how they found each other, Albert thought.

He browsed his newspapers, the local ones particularly. Lots of village fetes and other local events including Doreen and Harold (whoever they were) celebrating their diamond wedding anniversary. Sadly very few scandalous stories. The local MP had been up to no good with a mystery blonde, a young woman from Wobble on the Marsh had been a victim of an attack and was recovering in hospital. Apparently she had been beaten round the head and thus far had no memory of the incident. Police were asking for witnesses to come forward. Another about an attempted robbery of a local post office.

Albert drank his tea before remembering the bar of chocolate in his pocket. He held it in his hand looking at it with such love in his eyes; he wanted to savour every bite. He unwrapped it, closed his eyes and was just about to taste that sweet chocolatey goodness when it was snatched out of his hand. Startled he opened his eyes and saw Mary looking sheepish.

"Sorry Albert, Rose told me last night if I was to see you anywhere near anything sweet I was to confiscate it immediately. For your own good." She smirked and wandered off. Albert was in mild shock. That woman thought of everything! Surprised she hadn't already beat him to the shop and told the shopkeeper not to sell him any chocolate. No doubt that was coming. He still had to smile; he understood it was actually for his own good.

Mary came back shortly after with another pot of tea and with it half a rich tea biscuit. "It's on me," she said. Albert was grateful for the gesture, he knew however this might be his only biscuit for the next million years and would not be foolish enough to dip it into his tea and have half of it fall in, it was so small as it was. Instead he decided on the extreme and shoved the whole thing into his mouth.

From his seat he could see most of the village and collect his thoughts.

The view wasn't as good as their room at the Mad Cow but the tea was certainly better than whatever complimentary rubbish they had in their room.

He took out his pocket book and pen – keeping a pocket book in his coat was something that he never stopped doing after he left the police – and decided to make notes on everything they knew. So far they had lots of questions and very few answers. One thing he did know was that he was going to find out who Graham from The Mad Cow was meeting tomorrow at noon. In theory it was probably not relevant to what was happening to Patricia but his instincts and past experiences were telling him that there was no such thing as coincidence in a village this size.

Everybody was linked to everybody else in some way or other. He flicked through his pages of notes wondering what he should do next and how his Rosie was getting on and if she was struggling with all the questions like he was.

*

"So I told him to stick it back in his jeans and that I wouldn't even hang my ex-mother-in-law's towels on it!" Tracy said. This was followed by huge amounts of raucous cackling laughter from Rose, 'Trace' and "Chelle '. Rose had been intrigued by the two young girls wanting to set up business in a sleepy village (well that and the 50% off manicures sign that she spotted in their salon window as she walked past) and decided to go in.

The salon, appropriately named 'TrayChelles Beauty' was small but clean and nicely decorated. The walls were white with lots of mirrors and sharp pointy silver 'art'. There were a couple of black leather swivel chairs facing the mirrored walls where the girls 'did hair' and a couple of smaller rounded desks where they 'do beauty stuff'. This was where Rose sat now getting her manicure from 'Trace'. Michelle, currently without a client, had made them all tea and got out the hobnobs which the three of them munched on amongst their gossiping and was flicking through the latest copy of 'OMG! Did you see…?'

Rose made a mental note to omit the manicure receipt from their expenses. Rose loved gossip of course but decided it was time to start learning something about the village and its residents and more importantly just who had issues with the vicar's wife.

"So how long have you girls lived around here?" Rose asked faking conversation.

"Well I grew up here," Chelle said, flicking her long blond hair over her shoulders, "well until I was about ten when my mum left my dad and we moved away. This shop used to be my dad's, he was a butcher. After we moved away we had little contact, letters and birthday cards and Christmas cards and stuff but that's about it. He died years ago and randomly left me his shop. I met Trace at secondary school, been bessies ever since ain't we Trace?"

"That's right 'Chelle , the best of bessies."

"I brought Trace with me to come look at the place and then while we were here I had a mental idea didn't I Trace?"

"You did 'Chelle , well mental," she laughed.

"We were both at a loose end, just about to finish our beauty course and I thought 'Lets open a beauty salon!'"

"That's right, 'Let's open a beauty salon', she said those exact words to me not two feet from where we sit now," Trace was getting excited now and giving Rose a rather vigorous buffering, (obviously liked telling this story).

"Mum and me hadn't been getting on great and Trace had just split up with her boyfriend Jase, hadn't you Trace so we thought why not run away for a while to this sleepy old village and bring some life back into it." They all laughed.

"Not everyone approves of us and our fun party ways though do they 'Chelle?"

"No Trace that's right, that stuck up cow the vicar's wife for one, we only fell asleep in the churchyard that one time didn't we 'Chelle after one of Ponsonby's bashes. Admittedly we were spotted by half the bloody congregation on their way to church Sunday morning leant against some headstone or other. Honestly you'd have thought no one else had ever done that before the way Trisha went on. She might act like she's never had a day of fun in her life but there are definitely skeletons in that woman's closet you mark my words. Let's just say she's not your typical vicar's wife. Well Trace saw her in town didn't you Trace, more than once..." she began to say when a little old lady walked in the front door of the salon.

"Morning Mrs Jones." 'Chelle said walking over to her. "Let me take your coat, usual is it today, perm and rinse, lovely stuff," she said leading the old lady to one of the chairs. Rose couldn't fathom how on earth Mrs Jones could have a perm and rinse, there couldn't have been more than about three hairs on her head.

"Yeah so I saw Trish in town, in a café window with some bloke, on more than one occasion." Trace leaned in, her dark eyes were serious and her long bouncy red hair fell forward onto the table. "They were sat side by side, he had one of his arms round her and everything, thought she was getting romantic with him, even though he was some rough burly-looking bloke; then another time she handed him some envelope or other which he quickly shoved in his pocket, wandered off to the loo or something and I saw her scarper. Grabbed her stuff and practically ran out the café. Saw him come back from the loo and when he saw she was gone he got well angry. Was well weird. 'Chelle thinks it's well suspicious, got a bit of a bee in her bonnet about it and was dying to find out what it was all about. Couldn't care less meself, each to their own I say, none of our business really. There, all done," Trace said proudly admiring her work.

Rose had to admit she was very impressed too. She paid and thanked the girls and left smiling to herself. She could only admire Trace's each to their own attitude and although not very bright she could tell she was a good character. 'Chelle also was lovely but definitely had the brains out of the two. Rose couldn't really imagine her doing anything sinister though but she certainly wasn't as daft as Mary had made her out to be.

Rose strolled over to a nearby bench where she could gather her thoughts for a moment and admire her lovely nails. She was starting to feel peckish and would soon be meeting Albert in the park who would come armed with some more of Penny's pies. As she looked back at the salon contemplating what she had discovered, she spotted a chemist a few doors down.

Albert had been so good lately what with being a new diabetic and all. He had a terrible sweet tooth and although he was putting on a brave face she knew it was quite hard for him. She had read about some diabetic friendly chocolate that you could buy in the chemist so decided to pop in and see if they had any.

As Rose approached the counter she could again see the bespectacled lady with the tight bun and long skirt, Joyce, who had been in front of her in the queue at the post office.

"What on earth is taking so long?" Joyce said impatiently to the lady at the counter. "I can't leave mother for too long," she said angrily. "He should know that of all people," she said pointing towards a man that had just appeared from the back room. The chemist was surprisingly quite an attractive man, only in his late twenties perhaps, tall and slim with a ruggedly stubbled face.

"Calm down please Joyce," he said with a forced smile. "I'll take care of this Donna," he said and smiled at the other lady on the counter, who rolled her eyes. "I understand you are in a hurry but you must understand that your mother's medication has now changed and is quite a complicated cocktail now," he said handing her a large white paper bag.

"Yes I know that, I'm not stupid," she said harshly snatching the bag off him.

"I know you aren't stupid Joyce, but due to your mother's recent deterioration there are some very strong tablets in there and the timings and dosages have had to change as a result. I've written it out for you very clearly," he said handing her a piece of paper which she in turn snatched off him.

"I'm sorry Mr Goodsoul for being snappy. I'm very tired, haven't been sleeping very well lately."

"That's perfectly understandable, Joyce, given the circumstances. We can organise extra help for you if you would like," he said kindly.

"I can manage," she snapped again, then quieter, "I can manage thank you." He studied her for a moment before walking out from the counter to a nearby shelf.

"How about something to help you sleep then at least?" he said handing her a small box. She paused in front of him contemplating the sleeping pills before sighing and placing them in her bag muttering her quiet reluctant thank yous she left the chemist.

Rose felt for the girl. She too had had to care for her mother many years ago. She was only a teenager herself at the time and the strain was almost unbearable. Her sister Tulip wasn't much help, incredibly selfish for an older sister. She left home at eighteen leaving Rose, just fifteen to care for her mother. She had barely any contact with them and seemed to live eternally partying from what Rose heard.

It was soon after meeting Albert that her mother had died; he had been there at the end in a way that she could never repay him for, unlike her sister.

Other than an exchange of Christmas cards Rose and Tulip barely spoke again after the funeral. The last time Rose had seen her sister was seven years ago at her Aunt Margaret's funeral, even then only a few sentences were exchanged between them.

"May I help you?" The chemist's voice woke Rose from her daydream.

"I'm sorry," she said gathering herself. "I'm looking for diabetic chocolate for my husband." She smiled hopefully.

"Right over here," the dishy chemist said leading her to some shelves near the door. "We have a small range of chocolate and sugar free sweets available." He smiled again showing his pearly white teeth. He really was handsome; Rose could almost feel herself blushing when he smiled at her. She wasn't the only one too, she noticed a couple of other women in the shop ogling him not very discreetly. As he turned to walk back to the counter she said,

"I'm sorry, did I hear right? That lady called you Mr Goodsoul as in Reverend Goodsoul?" she enquired politely, accidentally fluttering her eyelashes as she went.

"Yes Peter is my big brother. I'm Jacob," he said extending his hand to her, "and you are?"

"Primrose, well Rose," she said shaking his hand for possibly slightly uncomfortably too long. "We are friends of George and Mary's visiting the village."

"Well it's very nice to meet you Rose," he said kindly, peeling his hand away from hers. "I hope you enjoy your visit to our little village."

Well besides the potential evil nasty blackmailer living in the village, what with amazing food, wine on expenses, manicures and dishy chemists she certainly would, Rose thought to herself and smiled.

*

After almost leaving the chemist without paying for Albert's diabetic chocolate then having to embarrassingly go back in and rectify the situation Rose made her way towards the park to meet Albert. She waved as she saw him sat on the bench armed with Penny's pies and two cups of take away tea. She plonked herself down on the bench next to him and gave him a peck on the cheek.

"Dying for a cuppa," she said gratefully taking it off him. They instantly began tucking into their pies which were again delicious.

Despite whatever her sister Denise might imply, Penny could do no wrong in Albert's eyes while she made pies like this.

Albert filled Rose in on the conversation he had overheard this morning, that Nigel was going to meet someone at noon tomorrow.

"Definitely sounds like he's having some sort of affair to me," Albert said with a mouth full of pie. "Not that I blame him considering his wife." They both chuckled. "Definitely want to follow him tomorrow though."

"It might not have anything to do with what we are here to do though Albert, wont it be a waste of time?"

"Nah, my instincts are telling me it's relevant just not sure why yet," he pondered. He went on to tell Rose about his embarrassing encounter with the reverend in the newsagent's where he purchased the saucy postcard to send home to Dave at which Rose laughed so much she nearly choked on her pie.

"So the reverend has invited us to dinner that's very kind. Must be careful what we say though, can't let him figure out why we are really here. Best check with Mary what story she has told him as to how we know them and rehearse it," Rose said with a hint of panic. Albert being ex-police could think on his feet and tell lies if necessary no problem (admittedly the reverend had thrown him earlier as he was not prepared) but Rose was not good at it at all. She was determined to try though, she didn't want to balls up their first real case when she had had to convince Albert to involve her rather than set up the private investigator business on his own in the first place.

He also told her about his trip to Mary's café, the very generous gift from George, and that she had given them the tea they were now drinking for free which was a 'result'.

"Then I went to Penny's pie stall over there," he nodded in the direction of the stall. "She apologised again for the little show with her sister yesterday and gave me these pies for free too!" he exclaimed.

Rose couldn't remember him being so excited in all their lives. They laughed and kept munching on their pies and when they had finished it was Rose's turn to tell Albert what she had discovered from her exploits that morning.

"Well first I went to the post office to get some stamps to send off one of my 'Dear Doris' letters that I replied to this morning and George was there working away behind the counter." She paused to sip her tea. "The woman in front of me, younger than me, looked like a librarian, long skirt, flat shoes, big cardigan, that sort of thing, well I learned that her name is Joyce." She took another sip of her tea.

"Is that it?" Albert said. "I know it's your first bit of real detective work but I thought you'd do better than that," he laughed. She fake punched his arm.

"Let me finish, let me finish," she said. "Anyway Joyce's mother by all accounts is not very well at all and Joyce is her full time carer and according to George is struggling but refuses to accept help or put her mother in any sort of home." She sipped some more.

"And?" Albert said getting excited.

"Joyce's mother refuses to go into a home after what happened to her friend Maud i.e. the vicar's first wife, as she went in and never came out and Joyce and her mum seem pretty bitter about the whole thing."

"Yes but hating the thought of going into a home is one thing but that doesn't mean you would send your dead friend's husband's new wife hate mail."

"I know that Albert, but it's a connection. We don't yet know how Patricia and the reverend came to be a couple, maybe something happened between them before Maud had actually died," she suggested. "Anyway we need to do a bit more digging there. This Joyce is definitely angry and bitter at the world." The Nutters were quiet for a moment gathering their thoughts.

"So after that I went to the salon," Rose laughed.

"Beg your pardon?" Albert said, pretending he couldn't have possibly heard her right.

"I went to the salon I said, purely for research of course." Albert looked at her like he knew her better than that.

"Well alright you got me, they were doing a special on half price manicures but also I thought where better to get a bit of gossip at the same time," she smiled satisfactorily.

"Go on," Albert said. "This best be worth it," he smiled, not caring if it wasn't particularly. Other than his wife's weakness for handbags she didn't often splash out on herself.

"Well I learnt that 'Chelle and Trace don't get on great with the vicar's wife, especially since she found them both half unconscious asleep on a grave in the churchyard after one of that Ponsonby blokes parties and gave them a very public telling off." Albert couldn't help but laugh at this. Rose continued. "On top of that Trace told me she saw Trish in town one day with some bloke, thought they were having an affair or something but it turned a bit nasty, Trish handed him an envelope, he went to the loo or something, meanwhile she scarpered looking quite distressed apparently. He came back and was visibly angry that she had gone. Trace didn't see any more and isn't overly interested but 'Chelle seemed a little too interested if you know what I mean." Albert nodded.

"You have had a busy morning haven't you love?" he said to Rose. "I'm very impressed." She beamed at him, very proud of herself.

"Ooh!" Rose suddenly exclaimed. "I saw her again a bit later in the chemist," Rose said after a short silence.

"Who?" Albert said.

"That Joyce the librarian looking character. I popped in there to get a little treat for my Albie," she said handing him the diabetic chocolate bar from her handbag. Albert smiled at the kind gesture. "She was getting grumpy with the dishy chemist for being too slow with her mother's new pills."

"Dishy chemist?" Albert enquired.

"And not only that, after some tactical mind games with him, I also learnt that the dishy chemist is also the younger brother of Reverend Goodsoul."

"See that's the thing with villages," Albert said. "Everyone is related to bloody everyone somehow." There was another pause as they finished the remainder of their cups of tea.

"So just how dishy we talking here?" Albert said. Rose smiled and rolled her eyes. "Eat your choccie," she said kindly. "You've earned it." Albert unwrapped his diabetic chocolate bar quickly, took a huge bite and instantly wished he hadn't. He smiled lovingly at his wife who looked so pleased with herself as he politely ate the most disgusting chocolate bar he had ever tasted.

Chapter 8

Albert had retrieved his Polaroid instant camera from the car and as discreetly as possible the Nutters had spent the next hour or so discreetly taking pictures of various places and people in the village.

In many of them Rose pretended to be the intended target posing next to a tree or lamppost or shop sign while the real target blindly walked by behind them. Graham was in the alley alongside the pub, talking in hushed tones on his mobile again. Joyce had been spotted coming out of the corner shop loaded with bags. Trish and Mary had been snapped together in the window of Mary's café talking very seriously. They had a lovely shot of the Reverend Goodsoul looking a tad confused at the woman posing for a photo in his graveyard with her thumbs up. Managed to get Denise and Graham Jr in one picture too as Albert sat on one of the pub's picnic tables sipping his pint while Denise ordered Graham Jr to take the rubbish out. Other than 'Chelle and Trace of course, who saw the camera and insisted on posing with Rose outside their salon and complimenting her on her handsome 'chubby hubby'. A few other characters had not yet been snapped, the dishy chemist for one – much to Rose's disappointment although Albert said he was 'probably gay anyway' – and no sign of Ponsonby either. He probably only came out at night, like a vampire, Albert reckoned. One of those rich people that sleeps all day and parties all night.

Albert had brought a collapsible board that they could pin their notes, photographs and anything else of use to in order to get a clear look at the whole picture. When the Nutters returned to their room at The Mad Cow they could see that housekeeping had been done, the bedding had been changed, the tea and coffee sachets topped up and their shoes aligned neatly by the door where Albert, pleased with himself for remembering the big step down into the room, promptly tripped over them. Making a mental note to hide the board of notes under the bed when they left the room the Nutters set to work.

Mary had called ahead and told the Nutters to meet at the vicarage at seven o'clock.

She had told them that their cover story for Peter the reverend was that Rose and Mary had become friends at college where they apparently both studied catering. Mary had obviously put her skills to good use as she now ran a café whereas Rose was technically a mother and housewife, avid gardener and a part time local newspaper agony aunt. This of course wouldn't do so Rose decided to add private party catering to her fake CV for the evening making Sandra her business partner. Incidentally her dear friend Sandra Ramsbottom struggled to make toast without getting it horribly wrong according to Dave so the Nutters found the thought of her in catering extra amusing.

Albert was permitted to remain as Mr boring insurance salesman and make no mention of his previous profession in the police.

Before leaving for the lovely evening walk towards the vicarage Rose decided to reply to another of her Dear Doris letters. She fanned the remaining letters out and shut her eyes and asked Albert to pick one for her. They both mentally crossed their fingers hoping for an interesting read.

Dear Doris

I have been married for 50 years now to my lovely wife Mildred. We have always been very active, have had many holidays, have 2 dogs that we walk daily. However lately whereas I'm ready to embrace old age and settle down, Mildred refuses to accept that she is getting any older. In fact she has gone the other way. She has started dressing like a teenager in short skirts and high heels (which is very dangerous for someone in their seventies) whereas I like nothing more than my comfy cardigan and slippers. She's spending a fortune on anti-wrinkle creams which between you and me she is about 40 years too late to do anything about. She like to go out and socialise of an evening and drink lots where I get the same drunk effect if I stand up too quickly from my armchair. I try and keep up I really do, but she won't let me take the lift anymore or anything and when I use the stairs it takes me so long, I have to stop half way to catch my breath then can't remember if I was on my way up or way down the stairs! I love my wife dearly and to me she will always be the beautiful teenager I met on Bournemouth pier all those years ago. How can I get her to understand that it's ok to grow old gracefully and without giving her husband a heart attack in the process (unless that's secretly her plan!)?

Confused, Cyril 83, East Wobblington

Dear Cyril

Can I firstly congratulate you on what sounds like a long and happy marriage. I hope my husband and I make it to 50 years (although he might disagree lol). It is very important to keep active and I'm pleased to hear that you still walk the dogs every day. Too many people get old and die before their time through lack of exercise and motivation so it's important to keep this up for as long as possible.

Your wife seems to be having rather than a mid-life crisis some sort of senior citizen crisis. A woman's worst fear is getting old and wrinkly and your wife is no different. She needs lots of reassurance. You need to talk to her and explain that she is as beautiful to you now as the day you met and that will never change, but nobody in their seventies should wear mini-skirts and deep down your wife knows this too.

You are a bit older than her and she also needs to understand and respect that. Although in mind you are both teenagers, sadly in body that is no longer true. Try to meet her half way in terms of being active, maybe an evening dance class at the local village hall which should be gentle and fun *for both of you. Or a few nice meals out rather than her teenage boozy nights or nights falling asleep in front of the TV. You both must be experts in the art of compromise and communication if you have lasted this long as a married couple. Don't let that stop now when it is still so important.*

Your friend, Doris

The Nutters took a gentle stroll through the village towards the vicarage. Albert popped in the corner shop to grab a nice bottle of wine to take to dinner where he spotted the elusive Mr Ponsonby-Gables, also checking out the wine. Albert picked up a bottle of reasonably priced red wine and checked out the label.

"Wouldn't pour that on my plant pots," Ponsonby said rather snootily. "Here try this one," he said handing him a bottle from a higher shelf that was four times the price. "Goes down like a whore's knickers," he winked at Albert and walked off towards the counter with his expensive wine purchase.

Charming bloke, Albert thought to himself. Odd use of the word 'whore' too, Albert noted thinking back to Trish's hate mail calling her a 'Babylonian Whore' not a word used very much these days. Albert pretended to wander around the shop a bit until Ponsonby had left before putting back the expensive wine and picking up the fiver-a-bottle stuff he had previously chosen. Rose would have gone nuts if he'd brought that wine, not to mention he wouldn't want to share wine of that price with anyone (he would make sure he drank the whole bloody bottle!)

"He's a charmer," Albert said to Rose as he left the shop. Rose had been waiting outside on the bench admiring the village. He relayed to Rose his conversation with Ponsonby and she was also not impressed. Rose suddenly panicked.

"You didn't buy that wine he suggested did you?"

"God no," Albert laughed, "I haven't got a death wish." They laughed together as they began the walk to the vicarage.

"Saw that Graham Junior lurking just now," Rose said. "Looked like he was waiting for somebody by the pub alleyway. I gave him a wave and he practically ran away, strange boy."

The Nutters approached the vicarage door, took a deep breath then Rose rang the doorbell.

Trish answered the door, she smiled warmly at them but looked tired. She shook their hands and welcomed them in to her home.

"Something smells good," Albert said, to which she smiled again. "Please come through to the lounge," The reverend, George and Mary were already assembled. Mary was wearing a mauve flowered dress this time, her hair and make-up immaculate as always. George was wearing another lovely cardigan, this one a sort of pea green with white diamonds. They were very warmly greeted by all.

"You must be Rose," the reverend said shaking Rose's hand. "You are most welcome," he said shaking Albert's hand also. Albert remembering his incident earlier with the saucy postcard blushed. "Please let me get you a drink." The Reverend poured them both a generous glass of wine. With the six of them assembled he said,

"Can I make a toast. To old friends," he lifted his glass towards George and Mary, "and to new friends," indicating Albert and Rose. "I hope you have an enjoyable evening with us this evening, we are very pleased to have you." They really did feel exceptionally welcome here.

Pleasant conversation continued thereafter when they were interrupted.

"Is there anything else I can do for you, Reverend?" a sweet voice spoke from the doorway. Rose was startled to see that it was Joyce. She didn't think Joyce capable of speaking sweetly to anyone but the reverend even got a half smile from her.

"No thank you, Joyce," Trish answered sharply, instantly putting a stop to her smiling at the reverend. "Can you see yourself out?" she said, more of an order than a question. Joyce nodded to them then left the room. "Joyce is our part time housekeeper, Tuesday and Thursday mornings mostly," the reverend explained. "She helps Patricia keep the vicarage and church clean and tidy. She's a sweet girl," he said kindly. Trish rolled her eyes at this. Not sure about sweet but she was certainly sweet on the Reverend Peter.

"The starters are almost ready if you would like to make your way to the dining room. Peter will top up your glasses won't you Peter?" Trish said leaving the room.

*

After a rather stressful day at college Poppy Nutter was almost relieved to be going to work that evening. She enjoyed Monday evenings. It was always buy one get one free on fish and chips every Monday and the place was full of old people all wanting cups of tea but they were all lovely and left lots of tips, mainly Werthers Originals or mint humbugs but she appreciated the gesture just the same.

Old people tended to go to bed early though which meant she would be out sharp tonight. Her bed was already calling her.

She and Charlie had stayed up quite late last night, they had bacon sandwiches and ate chocolate watching some slasher horror film on the TV. They had to make use of the time while their parents were away although her mum was partial to a good slasher and her dad wouldn't care what he was watching if he had a bacon sandwich in his hands.

"We'll walk you down the road," Charlie said putting his coat on. "Poor Allan hasn't been out all day have you Allan?" Charlie said shaking Allan's lead. Allan, lying down on the couch had reluctantly opened one eye and seeing Charlie looking excited shaking his lead, yawned, stretched and dragged himself of the couch. "There's a good boy," Charlie and Poppy both made a fuss of him as they headed out the front door.

They took the same route back they had the previous night through the alley behind Maple Street. There was a playing field and park just past The Wobble Inn where Allan was allowed off his lead to run free, not that he usually bothered much though except when a Jack Russell would yap at him or bird squawk at him, then he'd run.

Charlie was just about to leave his sister when they both heard someone calling from across the street.

"Pops! Cooee Pops!"

Across the street were two girls around Poppy's age, both blonde and pretty in an Essex sort of way. It was Chantelle and Chardonnay, Poppy's best friends and Chantelle in particular was one of Charlie's biggest secret crushes.

Poppy waved to them and they rushed across the street, Chantelle stuffing her face with chips. Even talking with her mouth full of food Charlie still fancied her.

The three of them giggled and made dramatic hand gestures and talked so quickly Charlie couldn't really understand a word they were saying.

"I told her straight Pops, if she wants him that bad she can have him. I'm going out with his brother Saturday anyway and he's so much more mature ain't he, 'Telle?"

"Yeah Char, his brother's like way better anyway, plus he's got that convertible which well suits you."

"How about you 'Telle?" Poppy enquired, catching up on both her friends' hectic love lives. "How's Jordan?" she enquired. At the very mention of his name Chantelle burst into tears.

"Oh well done Pops," Chardonnay said putting an arm around her friend. "He dumped her again."

"Oh I didn't know," Poppy said kindly trying to comfort Chantelle also. "Why didn't you tell me?" she said slightly angrily to Chardonnay.

"Well I haven't had a bloody chance yet have I, it only happened this morning," Chantelle continued to wail in the background.

"You are way too good for him 'Telle," Poppy said. "How many more times are you going to let him dump you?"

"I know I know," Chantelle said between sobs. "I'm not taking him back this time though Pops, I'm not, I swear it." Poppy and Chardonnay exchanged a look that said they knew better. Chantelle and Jordan had been on again off again for about six years now, all through secondary school. He was a complete waste of space.

Charlie, uncomfortable by the whole conversation and the wailing girl in the street had attempted to step away from the group. Allan lying on the floor by this stage was less than impressed with the noise. As he stepped back though an old lady with her shopping trolley happened to be walking past and he banged into her.

"You stupid boy!" she shouted at him.

"I'm so sorry," Charlie said, so much for his subtle getaway. The girls were giggling.

"You blind or something boy?!" she continued. "You've got glasses on your face why don't you use them," she said and then swung her handbag at his head knocking his glasses wonkily.

"I'm really very, very, sorry," he said putting his glasses back on properly and wondering if his head might actually explode with how red he had gone.

"And is that your dog pooing there?" he spun round and could not believe it. There Allan was at a time like this doing a number two in the middle of the street. Chantelle and Chardonnay were now laughing hysterically. "Make sure you pick that up, I'm going to watch you pick it up or I'll report you. You youths are all the same." The old lady swung her bag at him again, continuing her barrage of humiliation. They were a responsible dog-owning family who always picked up after Allan but he had hoped sincerely to never have to pick up dog poo in the presence of two of the best looking girls he had ever met and had had crushes on for the last six years. Producing the poo bag from his jacket pocket and stepping towards Allan (who was now looking at him as if it had been he who had just pooed on the floor) bent down to pick it up. Sadly in doing so he managed to put a finger straight through the bag. The laughter from the girls reaching new levels of hysteria and his face was now redder than a post box.

After cleaning poor Charlie up in The Wobble Inn toilet Poppy began work as usual. She smiled and waved at some of the regulars already in place eating their fish and chips special when she noticed on the back of the bar the wallet that had been left yesterday by the man with the limp. "Has this man not been back yet for his wallet?" she enquired politely to Felicity.

"Oh yes," she said. "He came back in and told us to leave it here behind the bar for him so he doesn't lose it again." She smiled at her own sarcasm. For all she was an intelligent girl, Poppy took a while to get sarcasm. Finally when it dawned on her she smiled.

"Oh you are funny, Mrs Bush," she said. "Have you rang him and told him we have it, there was some business cards inside."

"No I bloody haven't," she said. "I haven't had five minutes to myself today it's been manic!" Felicity always gave the impression she was the busiest most stressed woman in the world. "First we had the delivery this morning which we had to put away and then it turned out to be wrong, then I had to spend half an hour on the phone to them before they got it right and then I had to do the books and then the lunch time rush came and a busload of old biddies stopped in on their way to somewhere or other...." Her voice trailed off as she went off into the kitchen still talking to herself. Poppy rolled her eyes and opened up the man's wallet again studying his business card. At least it looked like a business card but didn't actually say what line of business he was in, just a name and a mobile number. She picked the phone off the wall that sat behind the bar and dialled.

*

The man was driving. He had to get back home and quickly. He had plans this evening, important plans and they included a woman, his favourite type of woman, one of copper hair and naivety.

Work had been terribly dull and tedious as it was every day for a man of his intelligence. His boss, a short mouthy little man who talked to him like he was a worthless idiot every day, had infuriated him yet again. If only he knew what he was capable of. Then he wouldn't dare speak to him like that. In fact, the man decided, he would let him have one more try at humiliation then he would let him know exactly what he was capable of. He smiled at the thought.

He was suddenly brought back from his fantasy of what he could do to his boss by the sound of his phone ringing. Not his actual phone obviously, this was his 'work' phone he liked to call it. He glanced down at the number and almost swerved with excitement into a new lane when he saw that it was The Wobble Inn's number. He had stored it earlier so he would know when the copper-haired waitress rang to tell him about his 'missing' wallet.

He was just about to pull over and answer it when he saw the blue lights of the police car behind him flashing and indicating for him to pull over. He couldn't believe it. Now of all the times. He so desperately wanted to answer his phone to the girl and now he was being pulled over. Why had he been pulled over? He wasn't even speeding. Frustratingly he pulled the car over as the phone stopped ringing, the answer machine cutting in. He watched the policeman approach in his rear view mirror. He wouldn't find anything in his car, he was always meticulous. He wound down the driver's side window and prepared to do his best false smile.

*

"Is there a problem officer?" the man said as warmly as he could.

"Couple of things actually," he said. "Did you know you had a brake light missing?" He couldn't believe it, he was always so careful so as to not draw attention to himself.

"No I didn't realise," he said apologetically. "I only had it MOT'd a few weeks ago, dammit," he said, faking frustration and shaking his head.

"I also noticed you swerved a little back there. Have you been drinking sir?" the policeman said, raising one eyebrow.

"Gosh no," he said putting a hand to his chest. "I never drink and drive officer I assure you. I swerved back there to avoid a squirrel," he lied. "I know you aren't supposed to but it's instinct isn't it?" he said. The policeman eyed him suspiciously.

"Well I'm sure that's the case but for my own peace of mind I'd like to breathalyse you please, sir. If you could step out of the car." The man was seething now; he didn't have time for this. He was in a hurry as it was and now this irritating policeman wanted to breathalyse him. He got out of the car and followed the policeman's instructions, assuring him that it would come back negative, which of course it did.

"Many thanks, sir. I'll let you off with a warning about your brake light, get it fixed immediately. They are so important on these country roads round here."

The policeman stood and watched the man drive away. He was a little jumpy, he thought to himself. Definite oddball. Was certainly in a hurry. He had made a note of the man's name and details when he did a check with the DVLA before pulling him over. Strange name he had, 'Ivan Oder'. Wait until he told his wife later, she'd think he made that up, he laughed to himself.

*

Poppy waited patiently, listening to the ringing of the man's phone until eventually the answer machine cut in. Must be at work or driving she supposed. She left the man, Mr Smith a kind message telling him who she was and that she had his wallet behind the bar of The Wobble Inn for when he was able to collect it.

*

Dave and Sandra Ramsbottom walked arm in arm through the village of Little Wobble. They had decided they fancied

The Wobble Inn's two for one fish and chip special for tea after Sandra – the worst cook in the world ever – had managed to burn their ham, egg and chips – this was with the ham being already cooked fresh from the butcher and the eggs still in the fridge not even having made it to the frying pan!

Dave thought Sandra did it on purpose personally because she couldn't be bothered but she was quite adamant that it was an accident.

The incident was especially amusing to them both after they had received a call from Rose earlier informing them that her and Sandra now had a fake catering business should they happen at any point to bump into the Reverend Goodsoul.

They talked about their days at work. Sandra was an estate agent and loved nothing more than showing keen happy, preferably rich people around their future homes. Today she had had a rather successful day selling a very expensive country second home to a wealthy gay couple, Martin and Cameron, who had already invited the Ramsbottoms to be their first dinner guests when they moved in.

Dave had had a pretty boring day, being a village policeman he didn't often get anything too juicy and scandalous to report.

A few bored youths had run away from him in the park as he approached them. He had spotted them spray painting various rude symbols and diagrams from the road and they had legged it as soon as he began to approach them. He ran after them for about ten feet, to show willing before stopping knowing he would never catch them. Not to mention the fact that he knew it was Gary Smith, the village mechanic's boy anyway so he had promptly informed his dad who had confiscated his computer, mobile phone and sent him back to the park with a tin of paint to fix it and a big sorry and thank you to Dave for not taking it any further.

Loony Mrs Jones had been in touch again. This time claiming she had been robbed of all her jewellery. When Dave arrived she was wearing about twenty necklaces round her neck and the rest of her jewellery was discovered in a saucepan on the stove. She gave Dave twenty pence, a button and a slice of fruit cake for his trouble.

Weirdest of all today though was the jumpy guy he had pulled over with the missing brake light. He was a fairly handsome middle aged man with a bit of a limp, he noticed when he asked him to get out of the car. He had been driving a bit erratically so he had breathalysed him then let him go. Particularly odd though was the copper-haired wig, ladies dress and shoes he saw poking out of a bag on the back seat.

Dave came to the conclusion that was why he was particularly jumpy, didn't want to be discovered with or worse, wearing women's clothes. Each to their own he supposed and sent him on his way. They laughed as they entered the door of their favourite pub. Greeted by Poppy's smiling face. She had poured their pint and gin and tonic before they had even reached the bar.

*

The man listened to the voicemail another time. She had such a lovely voice, the waitress, sounded genuinely sorry that he had lost his wallet, reassuring him it was safe and sound. He was still angry that he had missed her call. That stupid policeman stopping him for no reason. Probably not got anything better to do. He would have to be careful though, he mustn't draw attention to himself like that. He was usually so careful.

He had gone straight to the nearest garage for a bulb and fit it straight away, checking all of his other lights and tyre pressures at the same time. Tonight he had plans that could not be interrupted and he certainly could not risk getting pulled over on the way home. He was sorry that he couldn't speak directly to the waitress but at least this way he could save her voice and listen to it over and over and over again. She would have to wait her turn though. First it was someone else's turn.

*

Trace had been so nervous before the date she had drunk an entire bottle of wine before she had even left home. Don't get her wrong she had enough admirers, that sweet ginger boy in particular she knew was besotted with her but she just didn't see him like that.

'Chelle had been a bit concerned and was surprised that she was getting a taxi rather than being picked up but each to their own. Already feeling squiffy she sat at the bar of the pub with yet another glass of wine staring at the door. She had never been to this pub before, a bit out in the sticks but it was nice and quiet, perhaps that's why he chose it. Was quite romantic really. She looked at her watch again, he was now fifteen minutes late and she had almost finished her large glass of wine. He wouldn't have stood her up would he? She suddenly panicked, what if he had? How embarrassing, she'd never been stood up in her life. She took a deep breath.

"Don't be silly Trace," she said to herself quietly. She would give him half an hour then ring a taxi she decided. 'Chelle would probably kill him, she smiled to herself. 'Chelle was very overprotective of her.

She had not had much luck with men. She had a good feeling about this one though. When he had asked her out she just couldn't believe it. Of all the girls he could have he had chosen her!

She couldn't cope with all the questions and she was so nervous as it was she had told 'Chelle she was meeting a friend for dinner which wasn't entirely a lie she supposed. She ordered another large wine and sighed deeply. She had a really good feeling about him. He wouldn't have stood her up surely, he must have had car trouble or something. Maybe she would give him another half hour. She took another large gulp of wine.

A few minutes later the door opened and he smiled apologetically at her. He was terribly handsome. He walked over to her quickly, smiling that famous smile. She had already forgiven him for being late. Now their date could really begin, he had some making up to do. It was going to be an unforgettable evening.

*

He had been sat in the car park for over half an hour. She wasn't the brightest this one, he sighed. He much preferred a challenge. This one had practically snatched his hands off when he asked her out. He hated women who were desperate. If she had bothered to look round the car park she would probably have noticed him. She had been far too busy checking her make up in the reflection of the pub door to look round.

He always kept his dates waiting, one of his techniques. After letting them panic and think they had been stood up for half an hour, the relief on their faces when he finally turned up meant he could get away with murder for the rest of the evening. Literally.

*

Rose and Albert had spent the evening so far lying about the success of Rose's catering business and the fact that her friend Sandra was 'holding the fort' while they were away and trying not to be surprised when they heard things like George had a son who lived in Australia and Mary and Trish both volunteered at the local women's shelter. Equally George got a slight kick under the table from Mary when he seemed surprised that his dear friends the Nutters had three children.

They hadn't learned very much with regards to their investigation though sadly. Rose downed her fifth large wine and decided to ask some questions.

"So Reverend how did you and Patricia meet?" She smiled, Albert held his breath.

"Well," he said taking Trish's hand, "I was married before to a lady called Maud who the people of this village knew very well. She became very sick and was sick for a long time. She had to go into respite for many many months. She was in a lot of pain but one of the things that made her life easier was the care she received there. Particularly the care of a young lady called Patricia," he said smiling at Trish. Trish looked at the floor. "Patricia was Maud's nurse and her favourite nurse at that. She made what Maud was going through so much easier on both of us and we became very close.

"After Maud died, I was very lonely for a while until I saw Patricia sat with my congregation some time after. She had come to see how I was doing, how I was coping. I had Joyce here to help me of course but ...," he trailed off. "We started to meet regularly for coffee, then for dinner. She started coming to church every Sunday and helping me hand out hymn books and volunteering to help within our community at the women's shelter.

"It wasn't until Patricia told me that she had been offered a job in Scotland that she was going to take that I realised how much I needed her. She had made me fall in love again, something I thought only happened once in a lifetime. When I contemplated life without her it just didn't make sense. I asked her to marry me and thank God every day that she said yes." He smiled again, squeezing his wife's hand. Trish smiled at him but looked embarrassed.

"That's a beautiful story," Rose said with a slight tear in her eye. Any more wine and she would almost certainly be sobbing, Albert thought.

He wondered why both Trish and Mary had failed to mention the fact that Trish cared for Maud on her death bed. Perhaps that was why there was clearly some resentment between Joyce and Trish. Rose wanted to ask George and Mary how they met also, tie up that little mystery then realised that they were fake 'long term friends' so she would already know the answer to that. She would have to find out another time.

When it was time to leave the Nutters were genuinely sorry to go. The food had been exquisite and the wine free flowing.

Besides the fact that Trish seemed on edge almost the entire night waiting for one of them to give the game away, all in all they thought they got away with it. Mary had seen them out at the door, they would stay behind to help Trish tidy up before walking home themselves. She thanked them for their discretion and waved them down the garden path.

The short walk back to The Mad Cow was more of a long stagger this time. Rose and Albert, linked arm in arm, wandered past the graveyard giggling. As they walked through the square they were brought soberly back by an ear splitting scream and could see flashing blue lights. A crowd had gathered in the entrance to the park. As they got closer they could tell the screams were coming from 'Chelle who seemed to be hysterical. She was being calmed down by Ponsonby and Denise, landlady of The Mad Cow.

A paramedic was leaning over somebody lying on the ground. As the Nutters got closer they could see it was Trace from the salon lying on the floor, a pool of blood spilling from her head.

*

Mr Bush had kindly let Poppy leave early again, much to Felicity Bush's disgust.

It was fairly quiet Monday evenings after the oldies had all been in for their two for one fish and chips and then rushed home for Corrie, cocoa and bed. Audrey and Mavis were her favourites. They were such sweet ladies. No cocoa and bed for them. They loved a brandy or twelve, pinched Mr Bush's bum regularly and always left a good tip.

They were always trying to set her up with some distant grandson or nephew or something or other. So far she had managed to avoid a blind date though. They were very lively and she hoped that she was that much fun when she was their age.

She took the same route home as before, using the alley behind Maple Street. It was a little eerie walking through the alley but was a definite short cut to home.

As she came out of the alley into Little Wobble Lane heading towards home she noticed the house was in darkness.

Charlie must have gone to a friends she presumed, playing on the computer probably.

As she got nearer she also noticed that the front gate was open. This was unusual as her mum was very particular about the gate always being shut, for two reasons really. The first is that it would swing in the wind and banged which her parents found hugely irritating when they were trying to sleep, and also that in order to maintain her status of best plumage and annoy Marjorie Floppington next door, the house must always look like it came from some kind of gardening catalogue which meant gate shut. Charlie must have left in a hurry and not closed it properly behind him; she rolled her eyes in general at teenage boys everywhere.

She rifled through her handbag to find her front door key as she walked down the path before noticing that the plant pots near the front step had been knocked over. Soil had spilled out onto the path and some of the pansies were squashed and bent and not smiling at all. "What on earth has happened here Charlie?" she thought to herself. Her mum would hit the roof when she found this. She would sort it out tomorrow she decided, she was far too tired to do it now. She would make Charlie sweep up the soil and get some replacement pansies, mum would never know.

Finally she found her key buried at the bottom of her bag. She went to put it in the lock but the door swung open slightly, it wasn't even shut properly. Charlie wasn't usually so irresponsible, what was going on? She stepped cautiously into the house, all in blackness and listened. Was that a noise she could hear? Allan should have greeted her at the door like he always does, where was he? Her heart was beginning to pound hard now. Something wasn't right. She noticed what looked like muddy footprints as she walked down the hallway towards the kitchen where she could hear some sort of rustling sound. "Get out Pops get out!" she thought to herself. If this was a horror film you would be screaming at the huge-breasted half-naked girl to run, run for her life and here she was tiptoeing into what could be a very dangerous situation. But that was ridiculous, serial killers tended not to roam the streets of Little

Wobble. The closest thing to murder to happen in their village had been when her dad had caught her snogging Jimmy Braithwaite when she was fourteen and he was nearly twenty. Poor Jimmy, don't think he's ever walked the same since. She could hear noises now coming from the kitchen and the pale glow of light. She pushed open the door, saw the glint of the knife in the man's hand and screamed!

Chapter 9

"Jesus Christ Harry what the hell are you doing here!?" Poppy screamed at her older brother punching him in the arm. The mad axe murderer she thought she saw in the kitchen was in fact her older brother Harry, looking slightly inebriated (typical student) and had clearly been raiding the fridge and was in the process of making a sandwich hence the gleaming knife. Allan was stood by his side waiting for the inevitable bits of ham to fall on the floor that so often happened when Harry drunkenly made a sandwich.

"Ow," he said rubbing his arm. "Thought I'd pop home and see the parentals. What's up? Normally you are pleased to see me." He swayed side to side slightly.

"Well normally you don't scare me half to death, why didn't you turn some lights on or something, I thought you were a bloody burglar or worse!" she said, her heart rate slowly returning to normal. With that Charlie came rushing through the door.

"I heard a scream," he said face full of fear, then upon seeing his older brother smiled.

"Hey Charlie!" Harry said grabbing his baby brother in a headlock and ruffling his already scruffy hair. Charlie was fond of his older brother but quite jealous of his looks and way with the ladies. Equally although he'd never admit it, Harry could talk his way out of (or into) anything but was secretly in awe of his younger brother and his enormous brain.

"What you doing here anyway?" Poppy said as she began to tidy up the bread and butter and ham that Harry appeared to have moulded into what resembled a sandwich.

"Been at R Wobs with Stacey, couldn't be arsed to go all the way back to Appleleaf when I've got a bed down the road and a full fridge and a lovely family to visit," he said grabbing both Poppy and Charlie round the neck in a sort of embrace. Harry got lovey dovey when he had been on the booze.

They were a pretty close family anyway. Their mum had cried her eyes out when he went to Appleleaf University, even though he was only half an hour away in the car. His independence lasted about a week, now he regularly came back every five minutes raiding the fridge, 'borrowing' money and crashing in his old bed if he had been nearby. R Wob's, is the only nightclub within what feels like a million miles of Little Wobble and is very popular with local youngsters, not that they don't also enjoy the cheesy bands that sing at The Wobble Inn the last Saturday of every month. The siblings went into the lounge and flopped on the couch.

"Right then, who's up for a slasher flick?" Harry said.

By the time Charlie had put a DVD in and Poppy had returned from the kitchen with fizzy pop and popcorn, Harry was snoring. So was Allan, for a change.

*

The man sat is his car parked down the street from number 42 Little Wobble Lane. His evening antics had meant that unfortunately he had not been able to spend more time with the copper-haired waitress. He just caught a glimpse as she had drawn the curtains but that was enough for now. He wanted her badly and knew that she would be the best, the most satisfying.

He needed to feel what he had felt all those years ago again when he had finally got rid of his wife. If only he could remember exactly what he did to make himself feel that euphoria. He had tried strangulation on some dumb teenage girl and although satisfying that hadn't had the same affect. Tonight he had tried a hammer. He smiled, remembering the look on her face when she realised Prince Charming was anything but. It had been fun seeing her face. The last one he had taken by surprise from the back and had no idea it was coming. He knew then that he would need to look into the eyes of his next victim.

He was desperate to recreate the pleasure felt when he had killed his wife, he had been drinking of course and on such a high he couldn't see clearly in his mind what he had done. She had been so beautiful and so obedient at first. That was until that meddling bitch got involved. He had soon put a stop to that of course. How he would love to get his hands on her now. If only he could remember her name.

Killing her was the only thought that would satisfy his hunger without actually killing his wife all over again. He wanted to do it right though which was why he was practicing his techniques. The police hadn't even linked any of the cases as the methods were all different which was working hugely in his favour.

He had panicked when that fat policeman had pulled him over earlier, fortunately he didn't check his boot. If all the police were that dumb then he had nothing to worry about. Once he had completed his task he would move on to pastures new. He had a plan and was going to see it through if it killed him.

February 1989

The man awoke from his slumber. He felt like he had been asleep for a week. He knew he was on the sofa, happened sometimes when he had had a late night.

He couldn't be bothered to go upstairs to his wife, pathetic she was. Nothing at all like when he met her, when he chose her. He gave her everything she wanted, paid for her fair and square, rescued her from that whore house. Out of all the women there he chose her and she wasn't even grateful. He could feel the anger overcome him, as it often did. Although he had found a way to relieve the tension.

His head was banging but still he reached down to the floor fumbling until he found his whisky bottle and brought it swiftly to his lips. He rubbed his head and dragged one leg off the sofa to touch the floor. What was that? He jumped, the floor was wet, he hadn't spilt his whisky had he. He rubbed his eyes and staggered off the couch towards the curtains. He could see daylight round the edges so knew it was morning but the curtains were thick and very expensive so blacked out the room, just the way he liked it. He stretched to pull the curtains open.

As the sunlight came streaming in through the windows it burned his eyes. He blinked and blinked, all he could see was stars. He turned round to face his living room, slowly it was coming back into focus. The floor was wet here too, what was going on? His wife would have to clean this up quickly. He looked down at his feet to see what on earth it was and froze. It was red. Blood red. He jumped back from the bloody puddle, his feet making bloody footprints on the carpet. He was frozen to the spot taking in the scene around him. He could see more bloody footprints from where he had walked over from the couch. The couch! He could see blood spattered all over the white leather couch and the arm chairs. The ceiling too, the walls, the lamps, the television was all covered in blood. He patted himself down checking that he was alright. That was when he found the knife. The large brown-handled kitchen knife. He had threatened her with it before of course but never actually used it, well only that one time.

Reality suddenly dawned on him, he froze wide eyed and dropped the knife. Had he done this? Had he finally flipped and given his stupid wife what she deserved? She wouldn't be the first of course but he didn't normally make so much mess.

His head was pounding, how much had he drunk last night? He ran up the stairs shouting his wife's name. The bed was still made. Neither of them had slept there. He slowly made his way back downstairs rubbing his head. He stood by the front door wondering what to do. Why couldn't he remember?

The ground felt different beneath his feet, what was it? The rug! There was a rug here that ran the length of the hallway, it was gone. This was looking bad. He opened the door to his left, the door that opened into their garage. He fumbled the wall hook for his keys where he always kept them and opened the boot. More blood, one of his wife's slippers and what appeared to be a clump of long red hair. He closed the boot and wandered back to the living room. He quickly closed the *curtains he had just opened, headed for the sofa and sat down reaching for the whisky bottle.*

He couldn't believe it. He had killed his wife. He wasn't surprised, it was something he had to do to relieve his anger, it had been a while since his last. He took a long swig of the whisky and laughed out loud. She didn't have any friends or family, nobody would come looking for her. He laughed some more. He felt more alive than he had ever felt in his life. He was still laughing as he went to fetch his wife's cleaning supplies.

Chapter 10

The residents of Upper Wobble were in shock. Nothing like this ever happened in their picturesque village. Graham and Denise invited the shocked residents into the pub for brandies to calm their nerves. It was just after closing time and they had locked the doors to the pub when the screams had been heard.

After leaving the home of Trish and the reverend in a jolly drunken mood, the Nutters had been shockingly brought back to sobriety. They sat on a table near the bar, as Denise came over with the brandy.

"Terrible business," she said shaking her head. "And right here on our doorstep, that poor girl." Denise seemed genuinely upset as she poured the Nutters considerably large brandies, think she had already had one or two herself to calm her nerves judging by the amount she was spilling. "Gosh!" she exclaimed "And here you are visitors to our little village, what on earth must you think of us! Ooh," she said with dread as she staggered away, "this could be very bad for business, very bad for business indeed."

"See she's got her priorities right," Albert said shaking his head. He reached for his wife's hands, she was shaking.

"She'll be alright Rosie. You heard what the police said, looks like whoever it was was interrupted so she has a fighting chance."

Trace had indeed been alive, barely. She had been taken to hospital with 'Chelle in the back of the ambulance, accompanying her best friend. 'Chelle's pain had been heart breaking, her screams were full of the pain of losing a loved one. They were more like sisters than friends. In just the short time she had spent with them this morning she had liked them both very much. They seemed to be the only people in this village who were honest about who they were. Rose wasn't a religious person but tonight she would say a silent prayer for Trace to pull through.

The police were questioning people inside and outside The Mad Cow.

Turns out Graham Jr had actually found the body. He was a strange jumpy sort of boy anyway, God knows what this would do to him. He sat on a stool at the bar with a blanket round him, also drinking a large brandy. For once his mother was fussing over him, trying to get him calm and warm rather than the usual barrage of nagging. His father however seemed very distant. He was stood behind the bar, holding a brandy in one hand staring into space as if in a daze. Denise had to ask him three times to hand her some dry roasted peanuts for their boy so he could eat something before he snapped out of it.

It was also surprising the amount of old people in their dressing gowns that appeared out of nowhere when they heard that free brandy was on offer. There had not been this many people outside just now, the Nutters noted.

"Nutter?" came a voice from behind them "Albert Nutter?" The Nutters turned round to see an overweight middle aged man with a bald head and grey moustache sporting a beige suit approaching them. Albert knew who it was before he turned round. That voice was extremely distinctive.

"Plonker?"

"Tonker, Nutter," the moustache said, swaggering towards them. "Detective Tonker now in fact," he smiled cockily at Albert.

Albert had been on the force with Bill Tonker, or Plonker as most people called him. They never had seen eye to eye. Albert was dedicated to the job and the people and doing what was best for the public whereas Tonker was a pencil pusher and would backstab anyone to get a promotion. He made so many mistakes he was laughable. He once turned up at someone's home address to tell a man his wife had sadly passed away. His wife incidentally then came out of the kitchen where she was washing dishes (very much alive) and punched him in the face. Plonker, rushing to do a job for the boss before anyone else could, had not double-checked the address and got the door number wrong.

He also got bashed on the head by an old lady that thought he was an intruder after entering the house next door to the house that had actually reported the intruder. He reminded Albert of those annoying swot-like children in school who would put their hand up to answer every question and give the teacher an apple every day and didn't have any friends. Dave still had to work with him now and frequently passed on more stories of Plonker's continuing incompetence. The fact that the man was now leading this investigation was quite a shock to Albert's system.

"What you doing here Nutter?" he said accusingly at Albert "Pretending you're a policeman?" he laughed at his own little joke very loudly.

"Yes Bill, very much like you," Albert muttered to Rose. "We are visiting friends in the village, staying here at The Mad Cow for a few days. That poor girl," he said shaking his head. "Any leads?" he enquired knowing that Tonker wouldn't give him anything.

"You know I can't discuss an open investigation with a member of the public, Nutter (emphasis on the word public) Have you forgotten everything you learned already? Honestly no wonder they kicked you out," he smirked trying to bait Albert. They had never seen eye to eye, he hadn't even been particularly kind when Albert had been stabbed by the mad clown. "Still got a fear of clowns have we?" he laughed out loud at his own joke as he began to walk away. Albert was devastated when his injury had meant he'd had to give up the job he so loved. It was cruel of Tonker to tease him this way.

"You know I was one of the first on the scene," Albert said. "If you bothered to ask, you should be questioning me as a witness? Do they still call you 'half a job' Plonker? And also shouldn't you put that brandy down," he said eyeing the brandy glass in his hand. Tonker went bright red and quickly put the glass down on the nearest table. "Drinking on the job," Albert said dramatically tutting and shaking his head, "hope you don't get breathalysed on the way to the headmaster's office." Rose couldn't help a smile. Tonker looked angry.

Some spotty faced policeman just out of nappies called "Sir" from the doorway, ushering Tonker over.

"Coming Smythe," he shouted back. "Urgent police business to attend to," he said then leaned over them. "Just leave the detective work to the real policemen Nutter," Tonker said, his large body swaggering away from them, bumping into a chair on the way out. Albert wasn't sure if he or Rose would punch him first.

The Nutters were awake early that morning. Nobody in the village had slept well that night at all, except maybe Denise considering the amount of brandy she had polished off.

They had learnt that Trace had taken a serious blow to the head with a blunt object, possibly a hammer. She had damage to the brain and had lost a lot of blood. The doctors had performed emergency surgery to ease the swelling on the brain and stop the bleeding and had put her into a medically induced coma to give her brain time to recover.

Until she was awake there was no way to know the extent of the damage but the good news was that she was alive. The police had taken statements from most of the village but so far there were no leads and no witnesses. In Plonker's own words, they had diddly squat.

The sun was again shining today and the birds still singing.

Albert could see crime scene tape from the window of their room in The Mad Cow and a policeman standing guard on the area. Rose got out of bed and joined him at the window. Both of them starkers but no one could see in so that was acceptable.

They saw Mary, today wearing a white and red polka dot dress and immaculate hair and make-up as usual, take a cup of tea to the policeman standing guard who took it appreciatively. A few young children in their school uniforms were trying to see round the policeman into the crime scene, their morbid curiosity getting the better of them. They soon ran off when he waved his handcuffs at them.

As the Nutters went downstairs to breakfast the usual hustle and bustle of the pub was quiet and sombre. Normally Denise could be heard shouting abuse at either her husband or son but today even she was keeping her mouth shut.

"How did you sleep?" she asked as if by habit then smiled sheepishly knowing that they had probably barely slept at all.

They ordered their breakfast, just cereal, tea and toast today. Even Albert had lost his appetite and couldn't stomach the huge fry up. Not only had they come to what looked like the most picturesque village in an English country catalogue to investigate vicious hate mail now they had a killer or attempted killer to contend with.

Albert knew from past experience that it was hard getting information out of people in a tight knit community at the best of times but now either they would all start clamming up and not give anything away or start pointing the finger publicly at each other which could tear the community apart.

"No Graham Jr this morning?" Albert enquired noticing his absence. By now he would normally have made his presence known by spilling something or dropping something and his mother shouting at him.

"No we've left him in bed the poor love," Denise said with actual motherly affection. "He's very shook up on account of him finding the body and all." She had told practically everyone she came across how her Graham Jr had come across the body.

"Not a body. It was Trace," Rose corrected her due to the fact that she wasn't actually dead.

"Of course, Trace. Finding Trace. Silly me," she said again rather sheepishly. Graham came out of the kitchen with their tea and toast at that moment, smiling politely as he placed it on their table.

"Popping out later this morning, after all the breakfasts, about ten-ish" he said coldly to his wife.

"What today?!" she exclaimed. "Surely we are going to be ridiculously busy with the gossips and journalists that are bound to turn up and Graham Jr not able to help today," she said angrily.

"I'll be back before we open at lunch time," he said sternly. So far Denise had proved to wear the trousers in this pub but something about the tone of his voice and the Nutters sat nearby made her keep quiet. Her face red she stood behind the bar, angrily wiping the same spot over and over with the dishcloth.

Albert made a mental note to return to The Mad Cow just before ten so that they could find out where he was going and who he was meeting.

Rose had admitted that based on recent events no stone was to be left unturned. Even if what they found him to be up to had nothing to do with Trish's situation there was a chance it would have something to do with Trace's and if they could help in anyway then they should.

Not to mention that Albert was even now twice the policeman Tonker would ever be and was not optimistic of him being able to solve a crossword let alone an attempted murder.

Rose and Albert had received a call from Trish after breakfast asking them to meet her at Mary's café. She sounded worried. Albert popped in the local shop to pick up his newspapers while Rose waited outside staring at the dishy chemist's bum as he opened up shop. She couldn't believe he was the younger brother of the reverend. He happened to turn round at that moment and caught her eye, smiled a huge pearly white smile and gave her a little wave. Rose and her beetroot face immediately turned round and pretended to read the post card advertisements in the shop window.

At that moment Albert returned with his papers. Trace's attack hadn't yet made the paper having happened so late last night but they were sure it would be the talk of the village for a long time yet.

The Nutters walked arm in arm towards Mary's café nodding at the young policeman standing guard on the crime scene who smiled bleakly. Albert remembered when he first started out as a policeman. Sadly there were lots of boring jobs that needed to be done. He had spent many an hour guarding a crime scene, waving at traffic, sitting with an old dead body in a care home until the coroner arrived, that sort of thing.

Mary's café was busier than usual. A few mums stood outside with their pushchairs having dropped their children to school, gossiping and speculating and shaking their heads. Inside Trish was leant against the counter talking quietly to Mary. As the reverend's wife she made an effort to be always presentable, dressing in a blue and white flowery dress and matching blue blazer. However she still looked very tired. The women immediately stopped talking as the Nutters approached the counter.

"Morning," Trish said glumly. Mary rubbed her friend's arm. "Take a seat over there," Mary said pointing to a table in the corner, "I'll bring some tea over. "You alright if I have a cuppa with my friends Fran?" Mary said to the young girl clearing a nearby table. She was a pretty girl, seemed fairly shy, about sixteen years old. "Of course, Mrs Smith, I'll be fine." She smiled kindly.

Trish and Mary joined them shortly after at the table sitting with their backs to the room. One armed with tea and the other with biscuits. Rose promptly slapped Albert's wrist as he went to take one.

"Absolutely awful business," Mary said. "Poor Trace," Trish shook her head.

"Poor thing. Had a few run-ins with the girls, bit wild for a small quiet village like this one if you know what I mean," she said to Rose and Albert, "Certainly never expected anything like this to happen though. Both of them are never shy about the amount of men they spend their time with and they get so drunk," she said disapprovingly, "was only a matter of time." She said these words with sorrow. She had obviously not approved of Trace and 'Chelle's lifestyle for some time but seemed genuinely sorry that this had happened.

"Don't worry about that now Trish, show them," Mary said nodding her head towards the Nutters. Trish seemed hesitant at first but then reached into her handbag and pulled out a white envelope.

"I received another letter this morning if you would like to see it," she said. Rose took the envelope cautiously. The look on Trish's face was evidence enough that it was not good news. The letter was again created with black and white and red headlines cut to pieces and glued to the paper haphazardly.

Perfect Patricia sat on the wall
Perfect Patricia will have a great fall
All of the women and all of the men
Will know exactly what you did then.
Do you know from behind you look very similar to the other whore. I wonder if your blood will be the same colour.

They all sat in silence for a minute, Rose and Albert re-read the letter several times.

"This sounds like a threat Trish, you need to go to the police with this," Rose said kindly.

"She won't," Mary interrupted. "I've said the same thing."

"I am not going to allow this person to ruin my husband's life. He has been through enough, he does not deserve humiliation and shame, and me too. My life now is a million miles away from what it was then or what it could have been and I'm not going to let some sad pathetic nutter take it away from me." She said angrily. "Pardon the expression," she added, apologising for using their surname. The Nutters nodded, it happened all the time. "Whoever is threatening to expose me didn't do that to Trace, they are just jumping on the band wagon trying to frighten me and it's not going to work." Mary sighed with what sounded like relief and smiled. So far Trish had been very defeatist and saddened by the whole thing but now she seemed to be getting her fight back.

"Albert?" Rose said, noticing that he had been quiet for some time now obviously thinking to himself. "What do you think?"

"I agree with Trish," he said rubbing his handsome stubbled face as if his brain was working in overdrive. "Whoever is doing this to Trish is not the same person that attacked poor Trace. An attack of that nature takes confidence and balls and quite frankly our hate mailer has neither. Literally. The act itself and the wording implies it is a female, a cowardly one at that. Can you really think of no one that could know your past and the fact that you live here now?"

Trish was silent for a while before speaking very carefully.

"I have done nothing but think for the last few weeks, it's the last thing I think of before I sleep and the first thing on my mind when I wake up. The only people as far as I'm concerned who know about my past are sat at this table." With that a smash came from behind them, making them all jump. It was Joyce stood at the counter. She appeared to have dropped her tea cup which had smashed all over the floor. Mary got up very quickly.

"Excuse me," she said rushing off to help clear up the mess. She seemed almost grateful for the chance to leave the table.

Joyce was beginning to get angry with the cup as if it was the cup's fault. She was an angry character. Fran quickly poured her a new one and led her to a table to calm her down while Mary picked the shards of white china up off the floor. Rose got the impression that Joyce probably didn't get the chance to sit down and have a cup of tea very often so it was no wonder she was upset.

The scene was interrupted by the quiet tinkle from the bell hanging over the café front door. Mr Ponsonby-Gables walked in holding the arm of 'Chelle leading her to a nearby table. The café went quiet.

'Chelle looked like she had been up all night. Ponsonby's suit however was as sharp as if it had just come out of the box. 'Chelle sat at the table as if in a daze. Ponsonby sort of patted her on the head before walking to the counter to meet Mary who still had her hands full of smashed tea cup.

"She's been at the hospital all night poor thing, hasn't slept a wink. I'm trying to get her to eat something then sending her home to get some rest."

"And Trace?" Mary said.

"She's stable. Nothing anyone can do for her right now except wait until she wakes up poor lamb. Fingers crossed she might know what happened but the docs said there is a chance she might not be able to speak let alone remember her attacker's face." Ponsonby seemed almost smug at this news. Smug because he might get off the hook or smug because he was the first to know and spread the gossip, the Nutters wondered. That was probably just his personality. Mary had told them that he was basically wealthy, bossy and smarmy. Ponsonby looked over to Fran, clicked his fingers, pointing to the table where 'Chelle sat and mouthed the word 'tea'. Albert and Rose were surprised that anyone had the nerve to be so rude, yet even more surprising was that she immediately left Joyce's side to get Ponsonby his tea.

The Nutters remained for a while with their thoughts, watching Ponsonby devour a full English and when 'Chelle would only barely nibble a slice of toast he polished off hers as well. He really was quite repulsive. Money clearly doesn't buy manners.

Trish had left a while ago but the Nutters were surprised to see the Reverend Goodsoul appear in the café. He made a beeline for 'Chelle and crouched down alongside her and placed a hand on hers and spoke quietly to her. She nodded at him and forced a smile and a thank you. With that he stood up and addressed the rest of the café.

"Hello everyone," he said kindly, "I'm sure you are all aware of what has happened to poor Trace. I'm reliably informed that she is fighting every step of the way and we would like to hold a candlelit vigil this evening at eight pm for anyone that would like to light a candle and say a prayer for her and offer our support to 'Chelle in this difficult time. You are all most welcome. My wife and I hope to see you there." With that he smiled kindly at the room, nodded to Albert and Rose and then to Mary before saying his goodbyes and hurrying off. He must have wanted 'Chelle's permission before he ran round the whole village.

Although not a religious man Albert had said there was something soothing and warm about a community getting together and praying for a miracle when tragedy had struck. As a policeman Albert had been to a few candlelit vigils both to support the families of victims of crime and in an investigative sense. Quite often where murder or kidnap or a serious attack had occurred the perpetrator would also attend anything like this playing the part of a concerned member of the community or all too often member of the victim's family. The worst one he had been to had been for a missing five year old girl, kidnapped from her own back garden. Sadly no amount of prayer and hope had brought her back.

He would certainly be on the lookout tonight for anyone acting particularly strangely, as he knew the police would be, Plonker included. Certainly Ponsonby needed looking at more closely. Albert looked over at Rose, he knew she knew what he was thinking. They were here to solve a problem for Trish but he wouldn't be able to leave until he had found Trace's attacker too.

Rose and Albert left the café and were waiting on one of the benches outside The Mad Cow. It was almost ten o'clock and they were waiting to follow the landlord of The Mad Cow, Graham. Moments later Graham emerged from the door to the side of the pub putting on his jacket and looking around the square before heading off west. The Nutters waited a moment before getting off the bench and beginning to wander nonchalantly behind him when Rose tugged Albert's sleeve.

"Albert look," she said pointing towards the pub. Graham Jr had also emerged out of the same door looking rather tired and dishevelled before also scanning the square and taking off in the same direction as his father. The Nutters looked at each other confused before taking off after the Grahams.

Seconds later Rose tugged at Albert's sleeve again and pointed to the pub. Denise had come out of the same pub side door and was putting her jacket on. She was angrily scanning the village before taking off in the same direction as both Grahams. This time the Nutters waited a moment longer almost expecting someone else to emerge from the pub, before following Graham who was now being followed by Graham Jr who was in turn being followed by Denise, the original Mad Cow .

They followed them as discreetly as possible away from the pub and through a few side streets which were just as picturesque as the village square. Rose admired some of the front gardens. Marjorie Floppington would be extremely jealous of some of these, Rose thought to herself.

They kept their distance and tried to be as subtle as possible. Rose and Albert had to occasionally stop to catch their breath as they weren't as fit as two Grahams and a Mad Cow. They came across a small wooden bridge that covered a stream, not much was beyond that from what they could tell except a wood with lots of trees and Ponsonby's manor on the hill.

"I just wanted some fresh air mum," came a pleading voice as they turned a corner. Denise had her son by the ear lobe and was leading him back towards them and home no doubt. "Do you have any idea how worried I've been Graham Jr?" she exclaimed. "Sneaking out the house like that! I nearly had a heart attack when I went to take you a cup of tea and you were gone. There's a killer on the loose."

Rose and Albert had jumped behind a row of bushes by this stage and watched as Denise dragged her boy home so that they didn't see them. They knew from Graham Jr's previous expressions that he wasn't just out for the fresh air but was definitely following his father in a very determined manner. Besides they were more concerned with what Graham senior was up to. Hopefully they hadn't lost him.

They waited until Denise's voice had died away in the distance before taking off again after Graham. They were in a wooded area on the outskirts of town now and had no choice but to follow the stone path before them as quickly as they could. The Nutters wondered who on earth he could be meeting out here in the wood. From the brief conversations that they had overheard it sounded like there were two other women in his life besides the Mad Cow. The first had threatened to tell his wife about his "indiscretion with a certain pillar of the community" and another he was "meeting at the usual place" and "looking forward to it."

The Nutters noticed the wooded area began to clear somewhat and a small children's play area appeared. There was a handful of mums here some with pushchairs, some running around with toddlers. They just spotted Graham going through a clearing on the other side of the park.

Through the clearing they came across a rather large stately home. It was a large brown Georgian looking building with peacocks walking the grounds. The grounds were full of people having picnics, eating ice creams; it really was a beautiful area. Graham seemed to look around himself and then quickly hurried into the house which from what they could tell was open to the public. Albert and Rose had no doubt he was here to meet somebody. They decided to enter the house being tourists visiting the area after all and were glad they did.

Inside the house contained marble floors and pillars, a large chandelier hung in the foyer. People were there looking at various paintings on the walls. Rose had been fascinated with old houses and always visited them when they came across them which bored Albert stiff but of course he did as he was told.

Rose became distracted by the art and the sights of the house, completely forgetting why they were there in the first place until Albert nudged her in the ribs. Graham was walking up the large marble staircase to the first floor. Once he was out of sight the Nutters followed. When they reached the first floor they could look down over the exquisite foyer and see more art and some beautiful antiques. Albert decided to not struggle dragging Rose along any longer so left her 'oohing' and 'aahing' over some painting or other.

A few people were on the floor having a look around but try as he might he couldn't see Graham. Where on earth had he gone? He could hear some laughter from a room at the end of the hall which had its doors shut and a sign outside which said 'Private'. He pushed the door open just a crack to see what was going on behind it. Graham was there and he certainly wasn't alone.

"What can you see Albert?" Rose whispered trying to lean round him to see through the crack. He stepped back from the door as quietly as possible to give Rose a quick look. The look on her face told him that she was as shocked as he was at what they were seeing!

Chapter 11

Rose and Albert had an early meal in the pub before getting ready for Trace's candlelit vigil. What they had seen previously fortunately had left them speechless as they did their best to act normal around Graham and Denise. The temperature had dropped somewhat and the wind had definitely picked up so they both wrapped up in their coats before heading out of the front door.

Graham and Denise had announced that they would be closing The Mad Cow at eight o'clock for an hour so that they too could go and pray for Trace.

Rose and Albert walked slowly through the square towards the church behind Graham senior, Jr and Denise. As they came towards the edge of the square near the church Rose let out a gasp.

The church was absolutely awash with bright twinkling flames. They stood for a while and took the scene in. It was one of the most beautiful things she had ever seen, there must have been hundreds of flames, twinkling like fireflies. People were everywhere, some silent watching the crowd, some praying to themselves, some smiling and exchanging stories of Trace. Rose couldn't help but let a tear trickle down one cheek. Albert held her hand tightly.

As they approached the door to the church, through the crowds, Trish was handing out candles to crowds and the reverend was then lighting them. They took a candle from Trish each who thanked them for coming and exchanged pleasantries with the Reverend Goodsoul as they entered the church.

The church inside was also heaving with people many sat in pews, some on their knees praying. They took a seat in a pew at the back, the same seats they had sat in Sunday on their first visit to the church. The stained glass window in front of them was flickering with colour amongst the candle's flames.

Rose found the entire thing extremely moving and sat in silence for some time, Albert couldn't remember her ever being so quiet.

Albert's police training began to kick in at this moment. He began to scan the crowds for anything unusual. About half way down on the opposite side to them sat 'Chelle. She was being comforted by some women, that he didn't recognise, friends he supposed. Ponsonby was nearby again, perhaps too involved for Albert's liking. He looked bored by the whole thing and kept checking his watch but as soon as he caught the eye of 'Chelle or someone else he put on a very concerned face. From time to time he handed 'Chelle his hip flask which she snatched and downed gratefully as if it would numb the pain.

Penny from the pie stall had been saying a prayer towards the front; she stood up and began walking down the aisle towards the front door of the church. She caught the eye of her sister Denise who scowled back at her, her husband looked at the floor. This was clearly a regular occurrence. What had happened between the sisters for them to hate each other so? Rose's sister was horrible and selfish but Rose still didn't hate her, his Rosie didn't have the ability to hate anyone. Her huge heart and the empathy and compassion that she showed to people was one of the things he loved the most about her. Don't get him wrong, if anyone hurt a member of her family then all that kindness would go out the window. At best she would call them an ambulance once she was finished with them.

Graham Jr was staring straight ahead at the eyes of Jesus on the cross on the stained-glass window. He almost looked hypnotised. He didn't even seem to be blinking. He was definitely a strange boy but an attempted murderer? Albert wasn't sure.

There was a little giggling coming from a crowd of women, Albert noticed the dishy chemist at the centre of it. He was shushing them to show respect and they all fluttered their eyelashes at him.

Albert didn't get it, yes he was handsome in a young Pierce Brosnan sort of way and he had teeth whiter than Simon Cowell's but surely kindness and integrity and the ability to crush a man with your bare hands were the things women looked for in a husband. Well Rose did at least. Thank God.

George and Mary entered the church arm in arm and walked slowly down the aisle, nodding at Rose and Albert and other members of the village that they recognised.

Albert and Rose decided to join the crowd that had gathered outside. As they exited the church, coming up the path was Joyce, her dark hair scraped back into a scruffy bun and she was pushing an older lady in a wheelchair. Presumably her frail mother. The woman in the wheelchair glared at Trish.

"How are you feeling Hilda?" Trish said to the lady in the wheelchair who ignored her but snatched a candle from her. Joyce wheeled her mother over Trish's toe before heading straight towards the reverend.

"You are so good and kind, Reverend, to do all this," Hilda said shaking his hand.

"Well my wife does most of the organising really," he said blushing.

"Nonsense, this community would fall apart without you. Maud would be so proud," she said glaring back at Trish who was rubbing her toe. She caught sight of Albert and Rose looking at her and rolled her eyes and gave a look that said this sort of thing happened all the time.

Also outside the church were a few policemen in uniform, DI Plonker and his spotty-faced sidekick who had called him over in the pub yesterday. The men in uniform were talking to people and making notes in their pocket books, occasionally reporting back to Plonker with little snippets of information. One of the men in uniform caught Albert's eye and came over to shake his hand.

"How's it going Scottie?" he said.

"Good Albert and you? Mrs Nutter." He nodded his cap towards Rose who smiled back. "Heard you were staying here. Don't suppose you saw or heard anything useful," Scottie said hopefully.

"Afraid not," Albert said genuinely sorry. He had been wondering if they had left the Goodsouls' just a few minutes earlier they might have seen or heard something or scared whoever it was away and Trace wouldn't be fighting for her life in a hospital bed. Albert had learned a long time ago that 'What if this' and 'What if that' and dwelling on things that cannot be changed could tear you up inside.

"The only thing we know," Scottie went on, "Trace told 'Chelle she was meeting a friend for dinner but she doesn't know who."

"Male or female?" Albert asked.

"Trace told her it was a girl friend but 'Chelle said judging by what she was wearing, the amount of perfume she used and bottle of wine she drank before she had even left she suspected it was probably a bloke. Trace was obviously lying but 'Chelle didn't want to push her, she would tell her when she wanted to."

"Do we know where they went?"

"Not yet. She didn't drive and she wasn't picked up. 'Chelle said she ordered a cab, guys have been ringing taxi firms to find out if she booked a taxi but so far nothing. In a village like this there are so many independent taxi companies finding which one she rang might take some time."

"Checked her phone?"

"The phone itself is missing, as is her handbag. You know how long it can take to get phone records. If this was murder then everything could move much quicker but at the moment Plonker just thinks it's a mugging gone wrong." Albert could tell Scottie wasn't happy with this though.

"What do you think?" he said to Scottie.

"He did quite a number on her Albert," Scottie said shaking his head. "If this was a mugging he would have grabbed the bag and run. Maybe shoved her or hit her once. Not bashed her round the head repeatedly. She was well drunk by that stage probably, bit of a lightweight, 'Chelle said. I think the beating was planned and taking the bag was an afterthought to make it look like a robbery. This was definitely personal."

"Where was 'Chelle?"

"Home alone. That Ponsonby bloke was one of the first on the scene, looking into him too," he whispered, "knocked her door and got her out of bed to see it. Pretty sure she's no suspect though. She seems genuinely devastated, plus no motive or none that we can find." Albert and Rose took in this new information. "Until Plonker gets off his high horse and realises there is more to this than meets the eye who knows what is going to happen. He might strike again and maybe even finish the job this time."

"Scottie, get over here now," Tonker's booming voice shouted. He was clearly not happy with him talking to Albert for so long. Scottie made his apologies and left the Nutters to their thoughts.

Ponsonby and 'Chelle emerged from the church closely followed by a pile of girls and the dishy chemist. In turn they all shook 'Chelle's hand or gave her a hug before slowly walking away. 'Chelle was a bit staggery. She had clearly been drinking. Trish went to 'Chelle.

"If there is anything we can do," she said kindly putting her hand out for 'Chelle to shake. 'Chelle did not take her hand but instead began to laugh manically.

"You don't care about us," she said raising her voice. "You probably think she deserved this because she's young and has fun and knows how to enjoy life."

"That's not fair, 'Chelle," Trish replied quietly.

"Well it's true isn't it?" she shouted, slurring. "You can say 'I told you so' now can't you, bet you are loving this." Trish looked at the ground.

"I understand your anger, 'Chelle, I really do. We are all praying for Trace's recovery, I can assure you I'm taking no pleasure from any of this."

"Huh! You think you're so perfect," she spat with such venom it surprised Rose and Albert. "Well I know what you are really, and Trace knew too!" Ponsonby began to take 'Chelle by the arm and usher her away.

"Come on 'Chelle, let's take you home."

"I know what you really are!" she continued to shout. "And all these people are going to know it too!" she shouted. Her voice trailing off as Ponsonby led her away.

The reverend, George and Mary were all trying to comfort Trish. She shrugged them off and waved her hands gesturing that everything was fine and she was fine and went back to handing out candles to the newcomers.

Rose knew what Trace had told her about seeing her with a man in town and 'Chelle being extremely interested in the details. Had 'Chelle pursued this and discovered the details of Trish's past. Was she the one sending Trish these letters? After tonight's display she was definitely the top of their suspect list.

*

He watched the scene carefully. He could see the candles flickering and the crowds gathering. Personally he couldn't see what the fuss was about. She was no one special. Shame he had been interrupted though and couldn't finish the job, while she was in a coma though he had time to figure out what he would do.

He had enjoyed the shouting display just now though. He hadn't seen that coming. Just as Trace hadn't seen it coming.

*

Rose and Albert had 'one for the road' in The Mad Cow. Although it had been closed for the candlelit vigil, the family had kindly offered the Nutters a nightcap before bed.

Graham Jr had made his excuses and gone off to bed quickly and they had sat for over an hour on stools at the bar with Denise and Graham. This had been the first time that the couple had been sombre and civil and even occasionally smiling at each other.

Denise was definitely hard work but Graham must love his wife despite his secrets. They knew he was clearly paying a blackmailer. From the calls and conversations that they had overheard, wouldn't coming clean be better than all this?

Albert and Rose did their best to keep up with Denise the brandy drinking machine but decided that they had best head off to bed before they fell asleep on the bar. Rose propped Albert up and giggling they headed up the stairs. Only one other couple was staying at The Mad Cow at the moment apart from them; they had been told but they still equally did the loud drunken giggling and shushing of each other on the way back to their room.

Rose retrieved the ridiculously oversized key ring from her handbag (was far too big to be put in Albert's pocket) and attempted to unlock the door. Albert again managed to forget about the steep step down into the room but this time got a bit of a run up and ended up face down on the bed rather than the floor. Both of them found this hilarious as you can imagine.

Rose shut the door of the room and they were plunged into blackness, she struggled to find a light switch and instead felt the wall to the bathroom where there was a conveniently placed pull cord. She pulled hard on the cord lighting up the bathroom with piercing white light. Blinking carefully she turned round to face the room and screamed.

Chapter 12

Albert immediately sobered up at Rose's scream and rushed into the bathroom.

"There!" Rose shouted. "In the bath!" Albert peered into the bath.

"Jesus Christ, Rose, I thought you'd found a body or something!" Staring at the Nutters like they were actual nutters was a fat long-legged spider. It was playing that game where if it stayed really still it thought no one could see it.

"I'd rather find a body than a spider, you know how much I hate them," Rose said rushing out of the bathroom to hide behind the door.

Albert shaking his head opened the bathroom window getting ready to throw it out.

"Is it dead yet?" came a frightened voice from behind the door.

"No I'm not killing it poor thing. It's probably had a heart attack anyway you coming in here and screaming at it. Bet even the spider thought there was a body in the room." The bathroom door opened a fraction and Rose threw in a magazine and plastic cup before slamming the door shut again. Albert picked them up shaking his head and scooped the little spider onto the magazine placing the cup on top of it. The spider knocked at the cup and tried to climb up it, falling off the sides like they do, before Albert flung it out the bathroom window.

Albert opened the bathroom door to find Rose in the bed with the covers pulled up to her eyes. Albert had known Rose singlehandedly fight off two dogs that had tried to attack Allan once and got herself quite nastily scarred in the process but show her a spider and she turned into a gibbering wreck.

"Is it gone?" she said hopefully.

"Yes love it's gone," he said kindly, slipping into bed beside her.

"My hero," she said as she kissed her husband goodnight and they snuggled beneath the covers.

*

'Chelle had woken to a banging headache and the hangover from hell. She remembered the candlelit vigil and groaned. She had been so touched at the turn out and just how many people in the village came to show their support. She had let her emotions get the better of her and made a scene.

She didn't like Trish, never had and hated the way she was so judgemental all the time as if she was so perfect. She would have to apologise of course, for appearances' sake. She knew Trish had secrets alright, most of the people in this village had secrets, but she didn't want them to come out just yet and not like this. She wanted to wipe that smile off her face but when the time was right. Right now she had to focus all her attention on Trace and her pulling through. She didn't know what she would do if Trace died. It had been them against the world for so long. She shuddered at the thought of being alone, again.

She heard a noise from one of the other rooms, Ponsonby had helped carry her home again. If it wasn't for the fact that he was rich and a laugh her and Trace wouldn't have anything to do with him. He was sleazy and smarmy and quite frankly a bit of a perv.

She suddenly realised that she was naked. She definitely hadn't undressed herself and Ponsonby was lazy and normally dragged her shoes off and left her on the sofa or on top of the bed, not carefully undressed her and put her in the bed properly. She looked to the pink armchair in the corner of her room, Trace had brought it for her a few Christmases ago, one of her favourite presents she had ever received. Normally she flung her clothes across it and stumbled into bed. Her clothes were on the chair alright but folded very carefully and neatly, almost creepily so. Whoever that was in her flat it wasn't Ponsonby.

She got out of bed and put her dressing gown on and quietly made her way down the hall towards the kitchen passing Trace's room on the way. The door was wide open but she had been keeping it shut on purpose. The police had had a good look round and she had wanted some form of privacy for Trace so had kept the door shut at all other times. She could hear the kettle boiling and then the toaster pop and the scraping of toast being buttered. She pushed the door to the kitchen open and breathed a sigh of relief.

"Oh it's you," she said smiling.

*

The three Nutter children were up early. Charlie had to go to school and Harry had been caught trying to sneak out this morning without tidying up the mess he had drunkenly created in the front garden last night, knocking over his mum's plant pots. Poppy had almost let him get away with it when he offered to put in a good word with his friend Greg who Poppy fancied hugely but decided the mess was too much even for a date with Greg.

"Morning Mrs Floppington," Harry had smiled at their loopy next door neighbour who was clearly delighting in the fact that her front garden was currently far superior to her neighbour's thanks to her drunken teenage son.

Marjorie smiled and waved at Harry. Marjorie had huge orange hair held up by an obscene amount of hairspray and thick red-framed spectacles. She wore very loud colours and currently was the only person in the world who still wore shell suits. This morning however, she was wearing a bright flowery jacket with white leggings and gold flip flops.

Marjorie had been their neighbour for twenty years. She had a very intense competitive streak especially where her home was concerned. She had been competing with Rose for years especially with gardening and village fete's baking competitions and even regularly at The Wobble Inn pub quiz. She gathered a team of equally grumpy spinsters to compete with Rose, Albert, Dave and Sandra who only went for the beer and fun anyway and still managed to beat them most times.

She also has a niece named Gert that she likes to compare to Poppy and try and rub it in how great she is and how clever she is and how well she is doing at university and is singlehandedly curing cancer, that sort of thing. The fact that she looked like the back end of a bus though gave Poppy the upper hand.

Unable to say a polite word to the female side of the Nutter clan, Marjorie did however flirt and giggle and blush and had been known to grope (especially at Christmas) the male members of the family. Including Allan. As a result Allan would run a mile whenever he saw her or heard her ear-splitting cackle of a laugh.

Right now she was having a good look at Harry's pert teenage bottom as he bent over to pick up the flower pots he had tripped over last night. She quickly went red and flustered and rushed back in doors when she looked up and caught Poppy's eye as she stood on the doorstep arms folded.

"Bloody woman," Poppy muttered, shaking her head. "It's not normal." Harry laughed at her.

"She's only human Pops," Harry said confidently. "I do work out you know." They both laughed as he proceeded to do various Mr Universe poses. Charlie soon came running out the door, toast in hand, late for school again. Somehow he managed to nearly strangle himself when the strap of his bag got caught on the gate on the way out. These things happened to Charlie lots, Poppy and Harry used to laugh. A lot. But now they just shrugged or rolled their eyes.

Harry continued to clear up his mess when Poppy noticed the car parked slightly down the road. She didn't recognise it as any of their neighbours but she had seen it a couple of times now. She thought no more of it, went back inside the house and continued getting ready for work.

*

The Nutters went down to breakfast early. They had both had a restless sleep, what with the vigil and Chelle's outburst on their minds along with Rose having mini-nightmares about huge giant hairy spiders getting into bed with her and stealing all the covers.

They had been informed by Denise that there was no reported change in Trace's condition. The doctors had her in an induced coma and would not take her out of it until the bleeding and swelling on the brain had subsided. It could be weeks before she came round and there was no guarantee what she would remember if anything. They were also reliably informed that the village gossip this morning according to Graham when he went to get his newspaper was centred around Chelle's outburst and people speculating what it was she was referring to when she said the whole village would know what Trish really was. His favourite suggestions included: a devil worshipper, an alien, a pole dancer, and a man. None of which any of them believed but found highly amusing nonetheless.

Albert and Rose looked at each other knowingly as they obviously knew about Trish's secret past, well as much as she was willing to let them know anyway. Trace had seen her in a café making what looked like a money transfer and an angry exchange but how could they tie that to her past? They would meet with Trish this morning first thing and find out what it was that Trace actually witnessed.

*

The Nutters sat in the Goodsoul's lounge tea in hand. Trish seemed to spend most of her life making tea for visitors, she was probably sick of it. She, like them, looked as if she had also had a restless night's sleep.

"My husband is out, he is very involved in the community. Joyce called this morning, her mother Hilda is feeling particularly unwell and wanted him to visit immediately."

"Oh gosh is it serious?" Rose said alarmed.

"No don't be daft, that woman always thinks she's dying, she'll outlive us all, trust me. Joyce does basically anything she can to spend time with my husband, she's obsessed. He doesn't see it, thinks I'm being silly." She sounded a little bitter.

"Anyway, obviously you want to talk about last night," she said knowingly. "I'm sorry you had to witness that, sorry half the village witnessed it too." She shook her head glumly. Albert and Rose chose not to interrupt and just let her speak.

"You know I've had quite a few run-ins with 'Chelle in the past. Not really Trace, she's a sweet girl, basically does whatever 'Chelle tells her to. Do you think she is the one sending me this mail?" she asked them.

"Do you?" Albert replied. Trish shrugged.

"I don't see why? I can't for the life of me figure out how she could possibly have found any of it out. Not to mention why bother?

"She's such a vain girl I can't see her giving two hoots about anyone else really. Whoever this is hasn't asked for money to keep quiet or anything which is more 'Chelle 's style if you ask me. Obviously she knows something or thinks she does otherwise she wouldn't have said anything."

"We heard from Trace that she saw you several times with a man in a café in town. Is it possible she thinks you're having an affair?"

"Oh god," Trish said and began to laugh. "Is that what she thinks?" She continued to laugh. "If only she knew."

"So you aren't having an affair then?" Albert said.

"God no!" she exclaimed. For a vicar's wife she wasn't too bothered about using the Lord's name in vain.

"Whatever you or this village might think of me, I love my husband, very much. I could never have dreamed of having a life like this twenty years ago." She gestured to their surroundings. "I have never and would never cheat on my husband." She seemed genuine, Rose and Albert believed her.

"So who was it then? The man in the café?" Albert said. Trish sighed.

"He was an old client," she said shortly. "From Ida's house of hell. A regular in fact. He nearly fell over when he heard I was a vicar's wife. I met with him a few times, as he threatened to tell my husband if I didn't. Initially he wanted, well you can imagine, in exchange for his silence, but of course that was ridiculous and never going to happen. In the end he accepted a rather large sum of cash and a polite word from an old friend that told him politely to never dare contact me again."

"An old friend?" Albert enquired.

"No one you need concern yourself with." She dismissed him.

"But surely both the 'old friend' and this bloke are potential suspects, that must have crossed your mind?"

"The man I paid off isn't capable of spelling let alone sending poetic mail to me, and the old friend is still my friend and I can assure you has nothing to do with any of this." The Nutters remained silent taking all of this new information in. They would never have imagined this strong woman that sat before them being bullied into that life by a manipulative woman named Ida.

"What about Ida? Is it possible she's part of this?" Rose said.

"No, she got cancer and died years ago. Poetic justice some might say." The three of them remained silent for a while sipping their tea.

"Thinking like a policeman for a minute," Albert began thoughtfully. "If 'Chelle thinks that you knew Trace had seen you with this man and she was going to tell your husband, that gives you motive, and despite the fact that you were here all evening with us, you may be approached as a potential suspect." From the look on Trish's face she hadn't considered that.

Albert joked afterwards with Rose that knowing how useless Plonker was he more than likely wouldn't have the initiative to actually get as far as Trish as a suspect, especially while he had the view that it wasn't personal but a robbery gone wrong. If 'Chelle in her anger went to him with what she knew though it might be enough for him to actually bother to pursue it.

They were in a little bit of a lull in the investigation so decided to go back to basics. They hadn't yet studied the letters of the letters (if that makes sense) so Albert sent Rose into the newsagents to buy a huge pile of any style of magazine she wanted which she happily did. The challenge would be to allow her to actually put the gossip magazines down so that she could compare them. She had 'thought outside the box' as it were and bought a variety of magazines, some sport, some gardening, some women's, some male ones too, even though they were quite sure they were looking for a woman.

They returned to The Mad Cow and went up to their room. Their bedding had been changed but other than that the room looked like it was in order. Albert was getting quite good at not falling down the step in the daylight too which was good news. Albert had taken to rolling up their case details containing photographs and clues and dates into a tube and putting it in the boot of the car every time they went out as they didn't want The Mad Cow staff to be aware of the real reason they were visiting Upper Wobble.

After retrieving it from the car they spread it out along with the pile of magazines and the letters that Trish had given them. The letters were crudely stuck on but were all black from being photocopies of the original. Obviously whoever was doing this had access to a photocopier which they thought might help them until they realised the post office had one that anyone could use for five pence a copy at their own leisure.

They split the magazine pile in two and set to work. They made huge amounts of notes and although Albert was used to this sort of work Rose couldn't help but let out a squeal of delight whenever she found a match.

"It's like I'm a real Miss Marple," she said, Albert smiling and rolling his eyes.

After a couple of hours solid comparison work with only the odd tea and wee stop the couple had a pretty good indication of who they were looking for. The female theory was reassured by the fact that no letters were found within the men's magazines so Albert put those to one side to make use of later. 'OMG! Did you see…?' and 'Rumours & Bloomers' – their daughter's favourites – definitely made an appearance, the exclamation mark and ampersand symbols particularly were apparent. Other matches included 'Geraldine's Greenfingers', a gardening magazine, 'New You Skinny Moo', a weekly diet club magazine that Rose was familiar with, another called 'Tropical Travels' and another about knitting were the ones identified so far.

They had to prepare for the fact that this person was buying random magazines for the letters only but it seemed a little odd for a person to buy the same magazines where letters were appearing in the early letters that Trish received months ago and also the same were in the latest letter.

The Nutters gave themselves a well-deserved pat on the back and decided to get ready for another yummy Mad Cow meal.

*

Poppy Nutter enjoyed her job at The Wobble Inn. She enjoyed easy Mondays with the oldies and their two for one fish and chips but her favourite night to work was Tuesdays for the weekly pub quiz. Her boss and the pub landlord Nigel prepared the questions every week and occasionally slipped her an answer or two, much to his wife's displeasure. "As long as that's all you are slipping her!" she fumes regularly, storming off dramatically.

Her mum and dad and Dave and Sandra had a team every week called the 'Wibble Wobbles' and although they only went to get drunk and have a laugh they were a surprisingly clever bunch and often won, much to the disgust of Marjorie Floppington and her bunch of serious lady friends called 'Marjorie's Masterminds'.

Poppy's favourite old ladies Audrey and Mavis also came in every quiz night. Their team name was '3 brandies and we're anybody's' which was both amusing and true. This week however Dave and Sandra invited them to join forces with them as they were two men down due to the Nutters being on a case so this evening the four of them became '3 brandies, 4 gin and tonics, 5 pints and we're anybody's Wibble Wobbles'.

Everyone had their drinks and was seated – in their usual seats of course, if anyone dared to sit at one of the regular teams' tables there would be hell to pay. Well hell in the form of evil glares of disgust from said team that had to sit somewhere else.

Nigel took to the small stage in the corner of the pub and tapped the microphone several times and said "one two one two" like people do for some reason. When he was satisfied he cleared his throat and began nervously like he always did.

"Question one. What did I have for lunch today?" He laughed at his own joke. The entire pub groaned collectively. Nigel made a similar bad joke every week at the quiz. Hadn't had a laugh yet. "Only joking," he guffawed. "Question one. What is the capital of Malawi?" This real question one resulted in an even bigger groan and a few unpleasant words escaped Dave's mouth.

*

The man was waiting patiently in his car outside The Wobble Inn. From the car he could see the comings and goings of the patrons.

His copper-haired waitress came outside occasionally to collect glasses that smokers had helpfully left outside so he was able to catch a glimpse of her. He imagined running his fingers through her soft hair, the smell of her skin. His leg began to twinge. Whenever he thought about his wife his bad leg began to ache as if he needed reminding. He did his best to disguise the limp she had given him, the one thing she had ever done to fight back. He made sure she didn't fight back again after that though. He smiled. He remembered it like it was yesterday.

He had heard from the nosy cow next door that his wife had been seen having coffee with that interfering friend after he had forbidden it. God what was her name? There had been a scuffle in the kitchen and he had thrown her onto the dining table and was about to teach her a lesson when she grabbed the brown handled knife and sunk it into his thigh. He didn't feel much pain as he had enough whisky in his system thank goodness and she was always weak so fortunately it hadn't gone in too deep.

The doctors said he was very lucky, much deeper and he could have lost so much blood it might have been fatal. What a freak accident they all said. She was so sorry, Amelia, so very sorry especially when he had finished with her. Ironically she never did see her interfering friend for coffee again. He laughed out loud to himself.

He checked his watch, it was almost closing time at The Wobble Inn. He would have to wait for everyone to leave then would rush the door in a dramatic panic to reclaim his wallet. And her.

*

Well that seemed like the last of them. The lights were pretty much all out. He had watched two silver haired ladies bickering as they got into the back of a taxi. He could just hear the end of a conversation. "I told you it was Russia," one was saying to the other. "Well you didn't say it loud enough Mavis obviously!" the other replied. The man rolled his eyes.

He waited a few minutes more until he was certain of little or no activity and headed for the door. She would be out any minute of that he was sure.

*

Sandra Ramsbottom sat at the far end of the bar away from the front door, with what could have been her tenth gin and tonic for all she knew. Having brought Felicity her token large vodka she knew that they were safe to stay for a late one.

They had just waved off Audrey and Mavis. The '3 brandies, 4 gin and tonics, 5 pints and we're anybody's Wibble Wobbles' team had been fairly unsuccessful with the quiz this evening, although they did get a free drink each and a box of jelly babies for winning the picture round. They were all sports stars and Dave knew them all.

Marjorie's Mastermind's or Marjorie's Menopausals as she and Rose called them, were rubbish at sport and not amused.

Sandra looked at her reflection in the mirror behind the bar, her bouffant looking a little haphazard to say the least. Dave was in the loo for about the millionth time. Poppy was just finishing up behind the bar, putting away glasses from the washer and she could hear Felicity calling poor Nigel various useless names as per usual because he got the answer to question twenty seven wrong.

"It was 1988!" she was shouting, Drunken vodka-based shouting not angry shouting, "The year we got married, I can't believe you don't remember that. We were in Tenerife on our honeymoon, I suppose you've blocked that bad memory out of your mind too," she fumed. "The honeymoon you ruined by getting sick incidentally!" she continued.

"It wasn't my fault I got sick," he replied

"Well it certainly wasn't mine," she said. "You chose to have the shrimp. Next you'll be telling me you don't remember when my birthday is." Poppy and Sandra laughed and rolled their eyes at each other, poor Nige. The Bushes went on like this all the time, but secretly couldn't imagine either of them being with anybody else.

Poppy wandered off round the other side of the bar towards the front door to lock it. She opened it first once more just in case she had missed some glasses outside and almost jumped out of her skin when in front of her was the silhouette of a man. As the light adjusted she could see that it was the man with the limp to collect his wallet.

"I'm so sorry," he said kindly, "I didn't mean to make you jump. I was hoping to reach you before you closed."

"Don't be silly," she said. "Please come in, I'll get it for you." The pub was dark and quiet, exactly as he was hoping. He waited quietly by the front door alcove where it was particularly dark.

He had a syringe in his pocket ready to subdue her. He didn't always need it but usually the girls he had gone for were walking home in deserted alley ways or through quiet parks at night not in a busy village pub at closing time.

He had never been so excited as he was this time though. There was one other he knew would be his ultimate but it was too early for her. Just one more he told himself. He had a good feeling about this one. What was taking her so long though, he wondered.

"Mr Smith?" her delicate voice came from the other side of the bar. "Mr Smith, come through," she called. This wasn't part of the plan, she was supposed to return to him in the dark recess by the door. He gingerly stepped through the alcove into the main bar area, trying hard to disguise his limp.

Poppy was behind the bar smiling, another lady with large messy hair sat at the far end of the bar and next to her a stool had a man's leather coat across it. God this wasn't the plan, he thought angrily to himself. Another woman suddenly appeared from a door out back behind the bar slopping the drink in her hand.

"We're closed, clear off," she said between sips.

"Mrs Bush, this is Mr Smith he has come to collect his wallet," Poppy said kindly.

"At this time of night!" Felicity exclaimed.

"My apologies I was just passing through, on my way home from work, I often work late and was hoping to make it before you closed," he lied and smiled at the three women through gritted teeth, trying his best to remain in the shadows.

"Well here it is," she said, flinging it at him down the bar. She was a charming lady, he thought to himself. "I'd take more care of my personal possessions if I were you. We all had a drink on you though," she laughed her strange cackle of a laugh. "Only joking," she said. With that Dave returned from the loo and began to put his jacket on. The man couldn't believe it, the same policeman that had pulled him over was here in this pub. What if he recognised him?

"Uh well thank you, goodnight," he said quickly heading for the door, putting his head down. Felicity followed him

"Bye bye then, we've all got beds to go to," she said, practically pushing him out of the front door, leaving him dazed and bewildered. This wasn't how this was supposed to go at all.

"Who was that?" Dave said. "He looks familiar."

"Some bloke who left his wallet behind," Sandra replied slurping the last of her gin and tonic. "Dave?" she said as he headed quickly for the door. He looked outside and could see no sign of the man. Maybe he imagined it, but he was sure it was the same man he had pulled over the previous day with the ladies' clothes and wig in his car.

"Was his name Oder?" he said to Poppy. "Ivan Oder?" All three women cackled at the name. "I'm serious," Dave said, rolling his eyes.

"Nah the stuff in his wallet said Smith," Poppy replied.

Odd, he thought, he really had thought it was him. Then again he didn't get a great look at him and he had had a few beers. He shook the thought off and helped Sandra off the stool; she was quite a short lady and needed help both on and off it which was no problem as Dave, like Albert was a great bear of a man.

*

The man sat in his car absolutely fuming. How on earth had those people been in the bar? He had waited and waited. How could he have been so stupid. A policeman no less! He must have recognised him, the man saw him come running out the pub door after him looking for him. Limp or no limp though he was a master of hiding and hiding quickly. He didn't see him, no one ever did. He would have to avoid The Wobble Inn in future for sure but what about the girl? He wanted her badly and was determined to get her.

*

Albert and Rose were stuffed. Yet again Graham Senior had outdone himself. They had both had homemade pate followed by beef bourguignon and several glasses of wine.

The pub was fairly busy and Albert and Rose had been able to discuss everything from Trish to Trace and to Dave and Sandra's shocking display at The Wobble Inn quiz, but they had still managed to get one over on Marjorie's Menopausals, Sandra had delighted in telling them when she called earlier.

Suddenly the front door to the pub burst open and in strutted Detective Inspector Plonker and his greasy sidekick Smythe looking round suspiciously at all the patrons.

"Evening Plonker," Albert said to him and Rose giggled.

"It's Tonker, Nutter, and don't distract me I'm on official real policeman's business here." Denise was behind the bar and Grahams Senior and Junior had emerged from the kitchen.

"What can we do for you Inspector?" Denise said in her politest voice. "Is there a break in the case?"

"You could say that yes," he said rather cockily. "Do you think your son could accompany us down the station to answer some questions?" he said rather sarcastically eyeing Graham Jr up.

"He's already answered all your questions and told you everything he knows," Denise said defensively.

"Oh no he hasn't," Tonker said knowingly. "Arrest him Smythe."

With that Graham Jr dropped the plates he was carrying and took off through the kitchen door, Smythe in hot pursuit. Tonker remained looking very smug indeed, ignoring Denise's pleas that he had made a mistake. Smythe returned very shortly after with Graham Jr in cuffs and the pair of them looking rather dishevelled. He was escorted out of the pub to gasps and shock from the village.

Chapter 13

Denise had wanted to go to the police station with Graham Jr but for once Graham pulled rank and insisted she stay at home. She had of course had too many brandies to drive for starters and was very emotional and would more than likely punch Detective Inspector Tonker in the face. Albert and Rose found the thought of that quite amusing but had to agree with Graham that it would make a bad situation worse.

Denise had made the customers leave and had been very upset. Once again the Nutters found themselves sitting drinking brandy after hours in The Mad Cow.

"He's a good boy my Graham," she said between sobs. "There is no way he would have hurt that girl." Rose and Albert were inclined to believe her. He was odd yes but seemed harmless enough. Appearances were often deceiving though. Albert had learned that the hard way when he arrested Colin Killoran the killer clown. He shuddered at the thought.

He had learned through Scottie that 'Chelle had told them Graham Jr was obsessed with Trace. He would follow her places, stare through the windows of the salon at her, send her flowers and letters, just wouldn't get the hint that she wasn't interested. According to 'Chelle she had said that she was starting to get really scared. What started as a schoolboy crush seemed now to be an obsession and she was really scared.

Plonker was coming round to the fact that it wasn't a mugging but personal now he had been handed a suspect on a plate. This along with the letters 'Chelle had given them and the fact that he had no alibi and had 'found the body' Plonker felt was enough to arrest him.

The Nutters had also learned that the young gangly ginger youngster that they put at seventeen at the oldest was actually in his late twenties!

"He's always been a shy and nervous boy, well I suppose he's not a boy anymore," Denise said as if reading their thoughts. "Did well at school but didn't have many friends you know," she said sadly. "He really is the kindest creature you could meet. Loves animals. Did you know he volunteers at the kennels? That's how he and Trace became friends, she does too you see, volunteer there," she said. Rose and Albert let her continue. "He walks the dogs for them and strokes and plays with the ones that nobody wants. He'd bring them all home if he could. The amount of strays he's brought home," she smiled sadly. "When he was six he brought a bird home once that had been attacked by a cat. Carried it all the way home from the park in his hands to us, was so upset for it. Graham and I knew it didn't stand a chance the poor thing, one of its wings was barely attached." Her eyes welled up. "We took it to the vet, he insisted, that we try." Rose felt for her. She was too a mother and couldn't imagine any of her children doing anything like this.

"Nobody with a heart that big could do this. Especially Trace. I know how he feels about her. Such a lovely girl. Not like that friend of hers," Denise said with a hint of anger. Seemed to be the general opinion in the village the Nutters had noticed. "Trace is one of the few people round here that actually likes my boy. I don't care what 'Chelle says. They were friends, he wasn't her stalker and she certainly is not scared of him.

There was only one other couple staying at The Mad Cow and based on recent events they decided to check out very quickly and very rudely the following morning.

Graham had got back in the early hours. Their solicitor was quite adamant that young Graham would be released. They had nothing concrete and could only hold him for twenty four hours. Graham Jr had of course maintained his innocence and that there had been some sort of mistake. Trace was his friend and he was devastated that this had happened to her and finding her was one of the most horrific experiences of his life. He was praying like they all were that she would pull through.

Tonker was being a plonker apparently. No change there then, Albert thought. Had Graham Jr in tears.

Until he was home Denise refused to do anything out of the ordinary and was acting as normal as possible. The pub had opened as usual and so far nobody had come in, not even the one or two regular old men that were usually on the doorstep when she opened waiting for a fry up.

A small crowd had gathered outside the pub on the opposite side of the road, pointing, judging and gossiping. Denise was pretending not to notice but they could tell she was hurt. Albert and Rose couldn't help feeling sorry for them. From Albert's past experiences, people were very quick to judge the parents of killers and occasionally that was valid. Killers often were brought up in abusive poor homes but there were many exceptions. Colin Killoran for one. He had been born evil Albert was sure of it. His mother had raised him alone when his father died when he was just a boy. She was a sweet loving mother who did everything in her power for him but even as a boy, she would tell later he was evil and she was frightened of him.

At that moment the front door to the pub opened. They all looked nervously towards the door. It was Penny from Penny's pies, Denise's sister.

"Come to gloat have you?" Denise said to her sharply.

"Don't be ridiculous Denise," she replied. "I wanted to see how you were all doing. I know we don't see eye to eye but if there is anything I can do to help," she said, she sounded genuine.

"We don't need help from you or anyone," she shouted angrily

"Alright Denise," Graham said intervening. "Thank you for the offer Penny. We'll let you know if we need anything."

"Which we won't," Denise said sharply. Penny sighed and turned to leave.

"I really don't know how we became this," she said sadly to her sister, "we used to be so close." Denise remained silent. "You need to stop pushing people away Denise, this place isn't exactly packed with your friends right now is it?" Albert and

Rose looked at each other both thinking the same thing. She had a point.

Primrose Nutter was good at a lot of things, however she had two pet hates, knitting and bingo. When Mary and Trish had asked her to come to their local 'Knit and Natter' club or 'Stitch and Bitch' as it was more commonly known, her face had dropped.

"It's not all knitting," Mary had said. "We have a couple of games of bingo too," she said hopefully. Rose died a little inside while Albert did his best to stifle his laughter.

"But I don't have anything to knit with," Rose had said stating the obvious.

"I have spares," Mary had said before Rose could argue that one, "and lots of wool."

Trish hosted this club once a week in the church hall and lots of women in the village came so she could have a good look at the sort of people Trish was surrounded by. Of course she would go, she would hate every single minute of it but she would go.

They knew from the magazine collection that their potential blackmailer had a passion for knitting so she must go and take notes on just who attended (on the condition Albert stopped laughing at her.) Also he had been ordered to do something useful with his time too, not spend it in the pub until she got back as per his first suggestion.

Rose arrived just after eleven at the church hall. When she got there she was surprised to see just how many women were there, many faces that she recognised from the village. Some she had seen in church that first day, others at the candlelit vigil and some from the pub or the shop. She was rather surprised to see Joyce there, looking as dowdy as ever. Her black pleated skirt coming down below her knees and she was wearing flat shoes with thick white socks and a long brown knitted cardigan. Rose wondered if she had knitted it herself in this very club. Beside her in her wheelchair sat Hilda her mother. The pair of them seemed to have already started the 'bitching' part and were scowling at Trish and Mary as they prepared cups of tea for people from a small kitchen area with a window, rather like a canteen.

"Rose!" Mary called her over. "Here have some tea and cake." She pointed to several large homemade cakes cut into slices on the counter top. "Trish makes the cakes herself, and supplies the tea and coffee for free. That's why certain unexpected members of the community turn up." She nodded towards Joyce and Hilda as if reading her mind from earlier. Free stuff and bingo and people forgot their animosity for five minutes. People were such hypocrites.

Small crowds had started to gather on the round tables dotted around the room. A few mums were there with their babies in pushchairs around one of the tables. A couple of old ladies wandered in slowly, grabbed the biggest slices of cake they physically could and joined Hilda and Joyce's table. Rose was also surprised to see a table of young girls, maybe early twenties.

"Knitting has gone full circle you know. It has actually become a rather fashionable hobby for youngsters in recent years," Mary said again as if reading her mind. "No surprise that 'Chelle's not here today I suppose," she continued.

"'Chelle comes to stitch and um I mean knit and natter?" Rose exclaimed correcting herself.

"Yes, and Trace," Mary indicated the two empty chairs around the table of youngsters. On discovering one of the magazines used in the hate mail was a knitting magazine, 'Chelle had dropped to the slightly less likely list but now she knew she came to stitch and bitch if anything the evidence was mounting up. Wait until she saw Albert!

A few more tables began filling up, a mixture of middle aged and older women. Penny from Penny's pies sat at one of the middle aged women's tables, gave Rose an embarrassed little smile after their morning encounter. Rose did a rough headcount of about thirty or so people, it was clearly quite a popular little club.

Mary led Rose to a table at the back that was currently empty and the two of them sat down, with their tea and Victoria sponge. Trish was serving the latecomers their tea.

Suddenly the room went very quiet and everyone looked to the door. Denise from The Mad Cow had turned up. Rose couldn't help but feel sorry for her as people began to glare and tut and shake their heads and she could hear "ooh the nerve" and "no shame" comments from around the room. Denise kept her cool and walked slowly with her head up towards Trish serving the tea. Trish poured Denise a tea without thinking and gave her a sympathetic smile along with a very big slice of chocolate cake which she accepted thankfully. She walked over to one of the middle aged ladies' tables.

"Morning," she said quietly to the table smiling painfully and was about to place her things down when one of the ladies lifted her bag and placed it on the empty seat. "This seat is taken," the lady said spitefully and looked away from her. She apologised and moved on to the next table where a similar thing happened. Rose's heart went out to her. Rose's bag incidentally was on the seat next to her, she moved it to the floor as Denise neared and said nice and loudly, scowling at the rest of the room, "This seat is free Denise." Denise gratefully sat down next to her. Rose could see she was holding back the tears. Gradually noise returned to the room as people's conversations resumed and the clicking sound of knitting needles.

"How are you Denise?" Trish said when she had joined them. "I can't imagine what you must be going through." As the vicar's wife Trish had a certain standing in the community and was often a friendly un-judging ear to the village. She had shown herself to be a kind understanding lady, but something had gone wrong with 'Chelle. There was certainly no love lost there.

"I'm fine," Denise said unconvincingly. "It's all a mistake, a big misunderstanding and my boy will be home by tea time later with a big apology from the police I'm quite sure," she said again unconvincingly. "My Graham is a good boy. A good boy."

*

After Albert had finished laughing hysterically at his wife's misfortune of being forced to both knit and play bingo – two of the things that she hated more than anything else in the world – he knew if he didn't do some work himself and have something interesting to report to her later he would be in big trouble.

Denise had gone out and left Graham in charge of the pub. There was another woman there Albert had seen behind the bar before (must be a part timer) but so far only one person had been in the pub.

Albert was thankful he didn't need to follow Graham again to see what he was up to; they had walked for miles that day and the shock of what they had seen would remain for some time. However they weren't the only ones who knew Graham's little secret, someone was blackmailing him and he seemed happier to pay up than have his wife find out which was probably a good idea knowing her demeanour.

He was just wondering what his next step would be when his mobile phone rang. Probably Rose wanting to be rescued or for him to sneak some booze to her to alleviate the boredom he chuckled to himself as he got the phone out of his pocket. Unknown number.

"Hello," he answered cautiously.

"Albert, its Scottie."

"Scottie mate, any news?"

"Albert you know I can't talk too much, Plonker will kill me if he finds out I'm talking to you."

"I appreciate the help Scottie, but don't get yourself in trouble, mate."

"I know, I know, I won't, it's just that I need your help. Plonker has made his mind up on the boy and I just don't buy it. He's stopping us exploring all the other avenues for now as he's so certain but I've managed to track down the taxi driver that picked Trace up for her date. He said he took her to a pub in the sticks called The Giddy Boat, do you know it?"

"Yeah I know it, proper middle of nowhere. I've driven past it but never been in it."

"Hmm me too," Scottie continued. "See the thing is right now Plonker won't let us waste time chasing leads as he is so sure Graham is guilty, which he may well be but for my own peace of mind maybe you could go check it out?"

"Definitely!" Albert replied a little too excited. The both of them not really sure who was doing who the favour but equally they were on the same side.

"It might lead to nothing," Scottie continued, "in which case I'll buy you a beer for wasting your time." He laughed.

"I'll hold you to that," Albert joined in.

Albert popped in the shop to get his papers before heading off in his car to The Giddy Boat. He had driven past it a number of times but never been in. It literally was in the middle of nowhere with nothing surrounding it but fields full of sheep.

The drive from Upper Wobble had taken just short of half an hour. Trace was picked up by the taxi driver around half seven and found by the ginger boy just after eleven. With a half hour drive each way that left Trace unaccounted for, for roughly two and a half hours. Incidentally, Albert enquired with Scottie if the taxi driver himself had an alibi which he did. His trips had been recorded by the cab company and customers corroborated his story.

He pulled into the gravel car park, it was early for a pub, and so far only one other car was there. He laughed to himself at Rose's reaction when he told her that he had been visiting pubs while she was being forced into knitting and bingo.

Inside the pub was fairly dingy. Old fashioned wallpaper and dark brown wooden tables and bar. Definitely the sort of place you might come if you wanted to go unnoticed. He could picture couples having affairs and meeting here for an illicit rendezvous, giggling and holding hands over wine and peanuts.

There was an old man sat down one end of the bar on a stool wearing a flat cap and rustling a newspaper. Albert thought maybe they came as standard from the brewery or something as literally every pub in England had one of these men. He smiled as he envisaged them coming out of some sort of factory already attached to the bar stool. He took a stool at the bar also, a few down from the old man, who quite frankly had a bit of a whiff.

The landlord behind the bar was already pouring a pint for the old man who in turn was counting his money in what looked like two pence pieces to pay for it. The landlord was probably in his fifties, fairly slim with silvering hair and a tea towel thrown over one shoulder in stereotypical pub fashion. Once he had re-counted the old man's two pence pieces and put them in the till he rolled his eyes a little at Albert apologetically as he approached.

"What can I get ya?" he said with a bit of a country accent and a crooked smile.

"I'll have a pint of the house special ale," Albert said without having a clue what it was. Dave and he had a bit of an ongoing bet as to who could try the most ales around the country, the stronger and stranger the name the better. The house ale in this instance was the 'Giddy Bottom' which Dave would be very jealous of indeed. Well unless it gave Albert a Giddy Bottom in which case Dave would laugh his socks off.

Albert sat there quietly for a little while sipping his pint very slowly and pretending to read the paper. Now he wasn't a policeman he couldn't just grab the man and demand information, he had to be more subtle than that.

As well as today's paper he had yesterday's Daily Wobble which contained Trace's picture along with an article. Incidentally he had just noticed the small photograph and name of the journalist who had written the article. Lisa Von-Winkleknicker. Rose knew Lisa from working at the Daily Wobble on the "Dear Doris" column. She was young, mouthy, rude and would sell her own mother for a good story.

Surprising that she hadn't appeared in the village yet though? She was quite the vulture. He opened it to this page and tsked and shook his head loudly as the landlord passed nearby.

"Can you believe it?" he said. "An attack like this on our doorstep, it's a miracle the girl is still alive." The landlord nodded in agreement and his face became a little smug in a similar way to Rose's when she knew some gossip and wanted you to try and pry it out of her.

"You know her then?" Albert said seeing his expression change.

"No no I wouldn't say I know her but she's been here a few times before, in fact," he leaned in towards Albert as if to whisper, "she was in here that very night." He touched the photograph of Trace in the paper right on the nose. What a prat this guy was, Albert thought, he was weird enough himself to be involved.

"No way," Albert whispered back excitedly playing along. This was too easy. This guy was obviously one of those that wanted to be the one in the know so he could give you the 'I know something you don't know' face. "Who was she with? Did you tell the police?"

"God no, I don't tell the police nuffin unless they ask. Have a very discreet establishment here if you know what I'm saying." He nodded towards a table behind Albert where a man was sitting alone and with that a woman arrived. Both of them wearing wedding rings and rather too passionately embracing for a married couple. Albert wasn't surprised, he knew it from the moment he laid eyes on the place.

"Besides, nothing to tell really." He straightened back up. "She sat on that stool there," pointing to the one next to Albert, "staring at the door, obviously waiting for somebody, wouldn't be the first time neither. Drank three large wines in about half an hour, pretty wobbly. I popped down to the cellar to change a barrel and when I came back she was gone. Just figured she gave up waiting for the bloke and went home."

*

When Rose and Albert met up again in The Mad Cow later that afternoon Rose had never looked so pleased to see him.

"Get me a drink," she said, "and the menu I'm starving." He knew she had more than likely had the morning from hell and at the moment she was not one to be argued with so he pecked her on the forehead smiled and went to the bar.

Besides the token old man who sat at the edge of the bar that came free with every pub, they were the only ones there. The village had decided to boycott the pub in protest since the arrest of Graham Jr. Albert had seen this sort of thing before, people were fickle and hypocritical though. They would be back as soon as Graham Jr got released. Then they would be all over them wanting the gossip and offering their false sympathies.

Albert had already told Scottie what he had learnt from the creepy landlord of The Giddy Boat and so over lunch he told Rose the story.

"No!" she said loudly with a mouthful of prawn sandwich. "And Plonker thinks it's not worth investigating? What an idiot," she said shaking her head. "How can he think that irrelevant? The weirdy landlord himself is worth checking out if you ask me," she said.

"I know, I thought that, but as weird as he is he was the only one working that night and the pub shuts at eleven so no way he could have got to Upper Wobble, bashed her on the head and got back to the Giddy Boat for last orders in the space of five minutes. The drive took me just under half an hour and I don't dawdle as you know." Rose nodded, that was true. Albert still drove like he was in a police car from time to time. Usually when they had a take away to pick up or when he had to get home from work instantly for Rose's amazing homemade three dip chips.

"Oh and another thing," he continued, getting the newspaper out and spreading it out on the table for Rose. "Did you see who's covering the Trace article?" he said pointing out Lisa Von-Winkleknicker's name to Rose. "Surprised she's not been seen here poking her nose about."

"She's supposed to be off, her granddad is really sick, on his death bed in hospital and they are really close. She's not leaving his side apparently. Came as a bit of a shock to us girls in the office, we didn't realise she was even capable of feelings. Family crisis and she still won't stop working though." Rose shook her head sadly.

"So," Albert said rather cautiously. "Dare I ask how your morning at stitch and bitch went?" he asked kindly and carefully.

Rose quietly so nobody could overhear her told Albert about the women blanking Denise and not letting her sit down.

"Honestly Albert I felt so sorry for her, you'd think she'd bashed Trace on the head the way they were going on. I made her sit with me, Mary and Trish in the end and tried to cheer her up a bit. She's just pretending that nothing has happened and that Graham Jr will be home by tea time the poor thing."

"Well according to Scottie they need something more substantial or Denise is right he might well be home for tea. At the moment it's all a bit circumstantial. He is definitely besotted with her, letters, flowers and gifts daily. Also he doesn't have an alibi prior to finding her and also a witness puts him kneeling by her stroking her hair before shouting for help but that could have been shock, but they don't have anything concrete enough to charge him yet Scottie doesn't reckon," Albert said between munching the ready salted crisps that came on the side of his sandwich.

"Well I did learn something interesting," Rose said a little smugly. "Apparently knitting is fashionable again and the club has a group of young girls that go regularly, two of whom happen to be 'Chelle and Trace." Albert nearly choked on a crisp. "I know that's what I thought," Rose said patting him on the back like it would help. "I almost took 'Chelle off the potential hate mailer list when we saw the knitting magazine in the collection but now who knows!" she said dramatically shrugging her shoulders. "So it wasn't a complete waste of a morning on my part." They both laughed.

"Ooh ooh ooh I almost forgot," she said excitedly reaching into her bag and pulling out firstly a small pile of coins. "I won one of the games of bingo! Can you believe it! I never win anything except The Wobble Inn quiz occasionally." Albert tried his best to congratulate his wife and share in her excitement even though her winnings consisted of one pound and sixty three pence bless her. "Aaaand," she continued, "I actually knit something." She handed him the smallest knitted thing he had ever seen. He took it and studied it. It looked rather like a tea cosy for the world's smallest tea pot.

"Wow," he said. "That's terrific." He tried to sound enthusiastic but after being unable to figure out what it was he had to ask. "What is it love?"

"Well it's a mobile phone holder of course," Rose said, grabbing Albert's phone off the table. "Look," she said excitedly as she tried to put the phone inside. Anyone with eyes could see that the phone was way too big for the 'holder'. His phone now resembled a fisherman with a knitted beanie hat. "See," she said proudly, then realising how funny it looked they both burst out laughing. Rose first, thank goodness, or Albert might have got a punch on the nose.

The village seemed happy to boycott The Mad Cow for lunch also since the arrest of Graham Jr so they had ordered pudding and an extra couple of drinks to drag it out and give the pub some custom for which they seemed grateful. Once they had dragged lunch out for as long as they could though they decided to go for a walk. A few people dotted around the village gave them a disapproving look, like they were friends with the enemy for staying at the inn.

Across the green they noticed Trish talking to someone over their garden fence; she looked up and caught their eye and waved them over. As they approached the house they could see that it was a lovely little cottage, with a front garden that Rose would have been proud of. Trish was on the path outside and Mary was on her hands and knees wearing gardening gloves carrying a little garden scoop. She appeared to be planting some bulbs into a little wooden wheelbarrow. Rose had a similar one in her front garden. The four of them exchanged greetings before Trish asked,

"How are Denise and Graham holding up?"

"Gosh I felt so sorry for Denise this morning," Mary said holding her chest in shock. "People can be so awful."

"Well they are pretending to be OK. The other guests checked out of the pub this morning and we were the only ones there for breakfast and lunch today," Rose said.

"That's terrible," Mary said. "Well we'll come in later wont we Trish," Mary said. "Join you both for dinner."

"Oh I don't know Mary, Peter is terribly busy," Trish began.

"Nonsense, I insist," Mary said quieting Trish. "We'll see you there at seven," she said firmly. They looked at Trish who smiled and nodded in reluctant agreement. They exchanged a few more conversational titbits before carrying on their walk, making a mental note of Mary's forceful nature and 'Greenfingers' as they went.

*

The man sat in his usual spot down the road from 42 Little Wobble Lane. He could see the waitress through her bedroom window at the front of the house, she was chatting on the phone laughing and smiling, brushing her long copper hair with her other hand. He had already seen her undress, seen her pink lacy underwear. She must have put it on just for him, known that it was his favourite. He had felt drawn to her the moment he had laid eyes on her, and although his attempts previously had been foiled he would not allow that to happen again.

Tonight he would relive his fantasy once more. She would never top Amelia though, obviously, but she just might set his mind at rest. He needed true fulfilment once more.

*

Poppy Nutter and her insane friends Chantelle and Chardonnay had decided to have a girl's night out.

Chantelle, still devastated over her fifteenth break up with 'Jordan' needed a night with the girls. Poppy was looking forward to it though. She had been working really hard lately and been really busy with college so she was looking forward to letting her hair down and drinking the drinks rather than serving them for a change.

The only club within miles was R Wobs which was a bit cheesy but still it was local and guaranteed some familiar faces. They would start at The Wobble Inn first of course, catch up on the real gossip and have a few cheap drinks – Nigel her boss would always sneak them free drinks, he drooled over her on a normal day but when she showed a bit of leg or cleavage, well you get the picture, and today she decided to go for both.

Poppy had her long beautiful hair in a high ponytail and put on her favourite little black dress. Her big brother Harry and his on/off girlfriend/bimbo Stacey were also going to R Wobs tonight and usually that meant amongst others his friend Greg would be there.

Poppy had had a huge crush on Greg for as long as she could remember but he never seemed interested. Well tonight with the little black dress would see to that. Her dad would have had a heart attack if he'd seen her in that dress, she smiled to herself as she left 42 Little Wobble Lane, being careful to shut the front gate behind her. She began tottering off down the road confidently in her ridiculously large heels, hoping nobody had noticed her slight ankle slip on the drain back there, how embarrassing.

"Hey Pops wait up!" a voice called from behind her. It was her baby brother Charlie scrambling to catch up to her while trying to put Allan's lead on. "We'll walk you down the road. I'm meeting Alex at the chippy he's coming back to watch a DVD with me later." Poppy laughed at him kindly knowing exactly why he wanted to walk her there. Hoping to catch a smile and a glimpse of Chantelle's cleavage no doubt.

As the front door to 42 Little Wobble Lane opened the man slid down further in his seat. She was so beautiful so elegant, so confident. He almost didn't notice her fall off her heels on the drain back there. He knew he had to wait, tonight it would be dark and she would almost definitely be inebriated, it was almost too easy yet somehow his attempts to have her were being thwarted by the most ridiculous of things. 'Aah here's one of them now,' he thought to himself as the boy, he guessed younger brother, chased after her with the ridiculously oversized dog, shutting his fingers in the gate as he went. He had never been scared of anything in his life but he was absolutely petrified of dogs. He turned the key in the ignition and slowly headed towards The Wobble Inn.

*

As Poppy, Charlie and Allan Nutter all walked through the alleyway shortcut that led to the pub they could already hear Chantelle and Chardonnay and more distinctly Chardonnay's huge cackle of a laugh. Allan rolled his eyes, much in the same way Albert did when he heard them coming. He recognised that sound and knew not only that it hurt his ears and brought on quite the headache, but face smooshing and coochie cooing from the girls would soon follow. Charlie gave Allan a look that told him if he pooped in front of Chantelle and Chardonnay again he would be sleeping in the garden. Allan gave him back a look that basically said he'd do what he bloody well liked, knowing full well that his mummy would go mad if she found out he'd been mistreated in even the slightest way. Once Charlie had been told off for not letting Allan through the door first! In jest obviously.

Chantelle and Chardonnay were climbing out of Chardonnay's dad's car, waving him off. They all shouted, "Bye Mr Char!" The three girls had the silly pet names for their dads, obviously Chardonnay's dad was Mr Char, Poppy's dad was Mr Pops and Chantelle's dad rather amusingly due to

Chantelle's surname being Stepley was Mr Step (although she couldn't understand why that was so funny).

After giving Allan various coochie coos and strokes and Charlie nearly having a heart attack when Chantelle dropped her handbag and bent over to pick it up, Charlie spotted his friend Alex outside the fish and chip shop. Alex was less comfortable around attractive women than Charlie was and Charlie was as smooth as sandpaper. So nervous in fact was Alex that he couldn't even come over and say hello but instead pretended he hadn't noticed them as he was reading the notices on the board outside the newsagents. The three girls tottered off together laughing into The Wobble Inn, Nigel the landlord (who came running out to 'collect glasses' the second he heard them) holding the door for them as they went and beaming from ear to ear.

*

Rose and Albert Nutter were the only people in The Mad Cow at tea time. Denise and Graham were pottering around as usual pretending that everything was fine even though their pub was empty. They had gone down to the bar a little before six o'clock to have a drink at the bar and wait for Mary, George, Trish and the Reverend Goodsoul to arrive.

Denise was furiously polishing the same section of the bar while staring at the front door. Graham was sat on a bar stool towards the end of the bar near the kitchen door staring at a pint. Denise seemed almost oblivious to them and continued to stare at the door. They stood at the bar for some time before Albert coughed a little loudly. Denise didn't react but Graham nearly fell off his stool.

"Gosh I'm so sorry I didn't see you there," he said sliding off the stool and rushing behind the bar. "What can I get you?" he said forcing a smile. They ordered their drinks and as he poured them he said, "Apologies for my wife. She's a little distracted. Our solicitor says that Graham Jr should be home this evening unless they find anything new, so fingers crossed."

"Please don't apologise," Rose said. "We understand don't we Albert?" He agreed. Graham smiled a sad smile.

"It's funny isn't it, you here complete strangers willing to accept us and this situation, yet an entire village of our so called friends and neighbours that we have known for years don't want to know us." It was sadly ironic, Albert had seen it many times during his police career.

"Will you be dining with us tonight?" Graham asked hopefully.

"Yes please, possibly four more joining us too," Rose said kindly. Graham nodded gratefully. They took a large round table that sat six in the middle of the room in an attempt to make it look busier and waited for the others to arrive.

It was still light outside on this warm summer's evening. Even now though the odd villager could be seen walking past, gossiping and shaking their heads in the direction of The Mad Cow.

They arrived shortly before seven, Albert and Rose on their third drink by now breathed a sigh of relief. They could hear some shouting coming from outside as they entered the pub. Obviously some locals had disagreed with their decision to dine at The Mad Cow. They could hear the reverend reply with various 'Innocent until proven guilty' and 'love thy neighbour' based comments. He seemed saddened by it all. Trish and Mary rolled their eyes almost apologetically.

"What must you think of our community?" Mary said.

"Ga ga ga good evening," George said greeting them warmly as he took Mary's coat for her. Immaculate as ever, Mary was wearing a slim fitting red dress this evening. The Reverend Goodsoul shook their hands with both of his again genuinely.

Denise seemed to come out of her trance, although disappointed it wasn't her son walking through the door she seemed grateful of the custom. They ordered two bottles of red and two bottles of white wine for the table and began looking at the menus while chatting cheerfully amongst themselves. Rose became slightly confused when the reverend asked her how her business partner got on at that catering function without her, completely forgetting her made up occupation thanks to Mary and Trish until Albert stopped her laughter by treading on her toe.

Denise resumed her place behind the bar polishing the same spot furiously again and staring at the door while her husband came over to take their order.

Shortly after Graham poked his head out of the kitchen and after his wife ignored several subtle loud whispers from him he threw a tea towel at her to get her out of her daze and indicated that she should help him in the kitchen. The pair of them returned carrying the table's starters between them. Albert had always been fascinated by skilled waiters and waitresses that managed to balance half the meals up their arms.

The door to the pub opened and the eight of them all span to look at the door, more shouty comments could be heard coming from outside as Penny and another woman Rose recognised as the lady that worked in the chemist came in. Denise's first reaction was anger until her husband touched her arm, and whispered something in her ear, her face softening. She went back behind the bar and although not smiling she was civil as she served them their drinks.

"On the house," Denise said, her way of saying thank you without saying thank you, before setting off towards the kitchen. Penny and the other lady stood there open mouthed before taking their drinks to a booth table near the window.

Shortly after two older men came in, the Nutters recognised them from previous evenings. They sat in the corner and played bridge, drinking ale pretty much every evening they had been in the village. Some angry voices again followed them in as the door opened, one of them shouting back quite rightly that 'he didn't care for gossip' and 'besides it was the only pub in the village'.

Considering Graham had other things on his mind the meal was done to perfection once again. Denise however, with one eye permanently fixed on the door, was steadying her nerves with one or two or three or was it four brandies? She brought more wine to the table without having taken the cork out, gave Trish a packet of peanuts rather than a glass of water like she'd asked and George's after dinner brandy coffee contained a blackcurrant flavour herbal tea bag.

Suddenly quite a row seemed to have broken out outside. They could see lots of people outside the window and hear lots of shouting aimed at a police car that had pulled up. With that the door opened and in walked or rather almost fell, Graham Jr. He was followed shortly after by Inspector Plonker and Smythe his greasy sidekick, both of whom looked furious. Graham Jr looked like he hadn't slept in days and had clearly been crying. Denise's brandies instantly left her system as she almost pole vaulted over the bar to reach her son, Graham senior shortly by their side. The family hugged for a long while, a tear running down Denise's face.

"We may not have enough to charge you yet boy but we will, rest assured," Plonker said.

"You've got no evidence, Inspector. Aren't you supposed to follow the clues rather than try and manipulate the evidence to the nearest suspect. Very lazy policing," Graham senior said sternly, the first time that they had heard him say anything with force ever. Plonker smirked before leaning into Graham Jr.

"I've got my eye on you boy," he said before heading for the door, Smythe following him like a puppy. The angry crowd outside seemed even angrier.

A bit later on Mr Ponsonby-Gables arrived. This shocked almost everyone in the room as he seemed to be very close to Trace and 'Chelle but by all accounts had the integrity of a drunken rabbit.

"What?" he said arrogantly. "They let you out didn't they old boy?" he said slapping Graham Jr on the back. "If I had a pound for every time the police brought me in for questioning," he laughed. "Especially where the ladies are involved," he said quietly, "well I'd probably be richer than I already am!" He laughed again really annoyingly loudly. Albert and Rose both rolled their eyes. "Innocent until proven guilty right, besides it's the only pub in the village," he continued, raising his eyebrows at Graham Jr who remained silent. "Drinks on me," he announced loudly. "And you two," he said pointing at Denise and her husband, "make sure you are jolly well at my shindig this weekend as invited."

Penny some time later walked past their table on her way back from the toilet. Being the only single looking women in the pub tonight Ponsonby had taken it upon himself to join her and the lady from the chemist much to their annoyance. Catching Rose's eye she stopped for a little chat on her way back to her table.

"Does everything he can to buy friends that one," she said, "thrives off gossip and scandal too. Doesn't give a rats toenail about Graham and Denise just wants them at his party to make it memorable and hopefully cause some sort of disruption."

"Yes we have been invited actually," Rose said sheepishly.

"Oh don't worry we all get invited, the whole village practically. Only go for the free booze and food obviously, he sulks if you don't go you see and he is our biggest village supporter. Any charity do, fete, after school club, you name it he sponsors it and in return we all have to pretend we like him and basically do as we are told." She shook her head sadly.

Chapter 14

The man watched the three girls stagger into the nightclub. He smiled to himself, this was almost going to be too easy.

He had checked the area out, he knew the route she would have to take to get to the nearest taxi rank. He had spotted an alleyway nearby where he could position himself out of sight. There were several large bins there that he would be able to hide between, be invisible. She would see him though. See into the deepest parts of his soul.

*

Poppy had decided to give up. She had done everything she could to get Greg's attention but had once again failed miserably. He would always see her just as Harry's little sister not a woman. He had paid her several compliments though, took great interest in her shoes particularly. Strange for a boy she thought?

Chantelle had already left, with Jordan surprise surprise. He had turned up at the club with some girl or other. Chantelle had caused a scene and ten minutes later was snogging him in the corner. Was all very confusing but it seemed to happen that way every time.

She finished the last of her Woo Woo and wandered over to the dance floor. Chardonnay was dancing with some dweeby looking boy of about seventeen. She had thrown Poppy the "rescue me" look several times now. She had, for her own amusement, ignored her for a few minutes until the dweeb grabbed her bottom then she had decided to go rescue her friend .

"Char I'm ready to go now."

"What?" the drunken boy said loudly. "But we've only just met," he slurred. "I think I love you," he said to Chardonnay pleadingly.

The girls both giggled and rolled their eyes walking away from the boy.

"Wait! Can I have your number?" he called after them which they ignored.

"You took your bloody time," Chardonnay said to Poppy.

"You looked like you were enjoying yourself," she replied both of them laughing.

"It's so hot in here, got to get out," Poppy said. They waved to the group and headed for the door.

"Ooh hang on I got to wee," Chardonnay said handing Poppy her bag, "I'll catch you up."

The cold air hit Poppy as she exited the club. It was surprisingly cool for a summer's evening but she needed it, she was hot and sweaty from the club. She started walking slowly towards the taxi rank. Chardonnay would catch up soon enough.

*

The man had seen her coming, his copper-haired waitress. From his position he was able to get ahead of her and position himself in the alley. He could hear the tap tap of her heels as she came nearer and nearer and hear her humming some song he didn't recognise to herself. What was that? He could hear someone else, besides the drunken smoking crowd outside the club he could hear someone else coming closer. He would have to strike now before it was too late.

*

Chardonnay in her huge heels was running down the street towards Poppy. Before Poppy could stop her she had overtaken her and stuck her head down the nearest alleyway and vomited. Loudly. Everywhere.

"I'm sorry Pops, the fresh air just hit me and I knew I shouldn't have had that blue shot, what on earth was that?" she said still hunched over. Poppy rubbed her friends back and grabbed her hair like all best friends do. She felt a bit queasy herself and this certainly wasn't helping. When Chardonnay was alright again the girls walked arm in arm towards the taxi rank.

"Come on Char lets go back to mine and order pizza, soak up some of that booze." They both laughed.

*

The man stood as still as he could, open mouthed. He could not believe what had just happened. That stupid little air head had thrown up right in front of him splashing his shoes!

He had ducked well out of sight and fortunately neither of them had seen him. What was it with this girl? Firstly the boy with the dog, then the policeman and now her friend practically throwing up on him!

He waited until they were gone and stepped out of the alleyway shaking his head in disbelief. It was almost as if he wasn't supposed to have her, but he wanted her so badly. He crossed the road and walked towards his car. He was getting his keys out of his pocket when something caught his eye on the village noticeboard. He walked towards it staring at the photograph and reading the article text alongside it. He laughed out loud. It was a sign. It was fate that he had met the copper-haired waitress, for she had led him straight to his ultimate prize and for that he would let her live. For now.

*

After yet another brandy based nightcap Denise and Graham finally let the Nutters go to bed.

They had closed slightly earlier than usual as the few people there for the night had gone home. All had had a drink on the house to celebrate Graham Jr's return but had all left by ten o'clock.

Albert had given his pal Scottie a call and had learnt that preliminary results on evidence at the scene, blood and hair was not a match to Graham Jr. The only thing he was guilty of was having a crush. Those that were in the pub took this news very well and word would no doubt begin to spread throughout the village of his innocence although in Albert's experience village folk were not very forgiving.

Albert and Rose had managed to successfully get back to their room without Albert falling down the step for once. Giggling the way slightly tipsy people do they climbed into bed. They soon dozed off.

Some time later they were awakened by a terrible crash from downstairs. The sound of breaking glass. Both of them sat bolt upright in bed.

"What on earth was that?" Rose said a quiver in her voice.

"I don't know," Albert said climbing out of bed and putting on his dressing gown. "But I'm going to find out."

"You can't go down there on your own," Rose whispered hoarsely. "What if it's burglars?" She too had got out of bed and grabbed her robe.

"Come with me then," he said sounding frustrated. "Just stay behind me."

"But I haven't got my face on," Rose said sounding horrified. Albert looked at her with mock disbelief.

"Potential burglars down there and you are worried about your face." He shook his head. "Besides don't worry, if anything you'll help scare 'em off." He laughed quietly. Rose proceeded to throw a pillow at him, he shhhhh'd her and opened the door to their room, peering into the blackened corridor. Well you've never seen two large people walk so daintily and quietly along a corridor and down some steps in your life. As they reached the bottom step Albert signalled to Rose to wait there while he checked it out, slowly pushing open the door to the main pub area as quiet as a mouse.

"Albert?" Rose whispered when he had been silent for a short time. "Albert?" she said again this time louder.

"It's alright Rose." She heard his voice, breathed a huge sigh of relief, not realising that she had not actually taken a breath since they had left the room. Rose pulled her robe tight around her and quietly crept into the pub after Albert.

The breeze hit her almost instantly, along with a crackle of something beneath her slippers. Denise, Graham and Graham

Jr were already in the room, staring in the same direction. A quiet tear was running down Denise's cheek. Someone had thrown a brick through the pub window.

Chapter 15

Daily Wobble journalist Lisa Von-Winkleknicker sat at the hospital bedside of her Grampy. He had been like a dad to her ever since her own dad had left when she was young and now he was leaving her too. She blinked back the tears. Her mum sat in the chair opposite sleeping. She knew this was going to be a difficult time for all of them.

She had her laptop with her and had managed to keep busy, she knew people thought she was heartless but it was just her way of dealing with things, keep busy and distracted.

The story of the girl being bashed on the head in Upper Wobble had helped for five minutes. Looked like a mugging gone wrong but still, the girl was young and pretty and things like that didn't happen in that village so she had heard. Still a scoop was a scoop. The girl Tracey something or other was in intensive care here in this very hospital.

Maybe she would take a walk to see her, she needed some air anyway. You never know there might be more to this story than meets the eye.

*

Graham Jr sat at Trace's hospital bedside holding her hand. They had got him wrong, the whole village had gotten everything about this so very wrong. He was in love with Trace, no denying that but he wasn't obsessed and he certainly wasn't her stalker. They were friends, the best of friends. He knew that she would never feel about him the way he felt about her, she was far too beautiful for him. He was tall and gangly with a ginger mop and glasses and she was just radiant. She was also far more intelligent than most of the village gave her credit for. Their days walking and playing with the dogs at the kennels were always his happiest.

He felt comfortable with her, they talked for hours, walked, had picnics. He had been her shoulder to cry on more times than he cared to remember when some man had broken her heart.

He could never tell her how he really felt about her, he knew it would ruin their friendship and he cherished that more than anything. He stared a while longer at Trace. He couldn't imagine harming her. He also knew he was a wimp and he had been bullied at school, unsurprisingly one of the reasons his mum fussed and worried so much but if he ever got his hands on the man that did this to his best friend then he wouldn't hesitate to kill him.

*

"What the hell are you doing?" a voice screamed at Graham Jr making him jump. He turned to the doorway of the hospital room. It was 'Chelle. She had that bloody Ponsonby with her, the charming chemist who he knew was anything but and some other girl whose name he couldn't remember all with her. They were all glaring at him.

"Get out!" 'Chelle shouted lunging for him "You put her in that bed how dare you visit her like this you sicko!" she screamed thumping him. He cowered covering his head with his arms.

"No I didn't 'Chelle! I didn't do this I could never," he tried to plead with her.

"Come on loser time to go," Jacob Goodsoul and Ponsonby grabbed him by the scruff of his neck ignoring his pleas and threw him out of the room, both of them smirking as they did so. The other woman was trying to calm 'Chelle down who could still be heard shouting as he ran from the ward.

*

Lisa Von-Winkleknicker came round the corner at just the right time holding the cheap nasty coffee she had got from the machine, to see the rich man and the handsome man throw the gangly ginger-haired man from the room. She had heard some of the shouting before too and had to jump out of the way as the boy ran past her clearly distressed. Nurses were running to the room trying to calm the situation and asking for quiet. They were in intensive care after all.

The police had arrested and released a suspect but all very quietly, plus she had been out of the loop being here by her Grampy's hospital bedside. Maybe she should venture out to Upper Wobble, just for an afternoon maybe? This might be much more than just a mugging gone wrong after all. She took out her mobile phone and smiling dialled her office.

Chapter 16

Albert did his best to reassure the landlord and landlady of The Mad Cow that this would all die down. People were hypocrites at the time but they have very short memories. Besides Ponsonby had a point, it was the only pub in the village after all.

Many people had come back to the pub accepting Graham Jr's release as his innocence but others were not convinced and continued to gossip and point and shake their heads at The Mad Cow family who in turn pretended that they didn't notice as best they could.

Graham Jr hadn't been seen all morning, gone for a walk to get some space his parents had said.

Albert and Rose had spent the majority of the morning discussing Trish and the hate mailer. They were getting distracted by Trace and the fact that they were getting paid expenses and eating like kings but really should get back to business.

From what they could tell and what they knew about Trish there was potentially loads of suspects.

They were pretty certain it was a woman from the style and the magazine letters being used. 'Chelle hated Trish but she seemed more the type that would blackmail if she knew anything. So far the hate mailer hadn't asked for anything to keep quiet. They were just getting off on knowing that they had the power to ruin Trish's life.

Joyce and her mother clearly hated Trish but they didn't make any effort to hide the fact so why bother writing letters when she practically told her every day anyway. Also how would she know anything about Trish's past. Mary knew though. She knew all about Trish's past and she certainly had the "Greenfingers" and knitting skills. Why go to all this trouble though? To do that to her best friend, Rose couldn't believe it, or didn't want to believe it. There was definitely a niggling there though in the back of her mind.

They headed downstairs around lunch time for a sandwich. An old couple sat in the corner munching some sort of salad, lettuce was hanging out of the old lady's mouth rather like a cow eating grass. When Graham Jr stormed back in looking very upset the pub stopped to stare. Denise and Graham were trying to comfort him but he wouldn't tell them why he was upset. Seconds later Inspector Tonker arrived with slimy Smythe looking very angry indeed.

"Inspector this is not a good time," Graham said sharply, annoyed that this man was in his pub again.

"We've received a complaint," Plonker replied very loudly. "You stay away from that girl and that hospital!" Plonker shouted at Graham Jr. "Do you hear me boy?" Albert, Rose, Denise and Graham all looked shocked.

"Oh Graham tell me you didn't," Denise said shaking her head.

"She's my friend mum. I just wanted to see her and see she was alright."

"Finish the job more like," Smythe muttered.

"I didn't do it!" Graham Jr replied frantically. "I'm innocent! Why won't you believe me!" he began to sob.

"Those tears won't work on me," Tonker continued. "While we may have had to release you temporarily we haven't given up on you yet my boy. You are still a suspect. If I find you near that hospital again I'll have your guts for garters!" Tonker shouted and he and Smythe turned to storm out of the pub. Albert could hear him still in the distance. "I want police protection on that girl's hospital room Smythe..." Albert looked like he was about to chase after Plonker but Rose held his arm firmly. Graham Jr ran upstairs to his room and slammed the door shut and the old lady in the corner shrugged and continued to munch on her lettuce leaves.

Lisa Von-Winkleknicker watched the chubby police inspector and his greasy looking sidekick storm out of the pub. She had stood ever so discreetly by the front door, pretending to be on the phone and making a mental note of every word.

She had been reluctant to leave her Grampy's bedside but her mum had insisted she get some fresh air and that his condition wouldn't change that dramatically in an afternoon and she was very glad that she did. Best not go in The Mad Cow just yet, don't think they would be in the mood for reporters. She spotted the café "Upper Wobble Buns" across the square. She could do with a decent cuppa. The coffee in the hospital coffee machine was revolting and stayed hot for all of about three seconds. Also a very good place to eavesdrop on the locals having a good old gossip, she thought to herself.

Lisa Von-Winkleknicker sat at a table in the far corner of Upper Wobble Buns with the best cup of tea she had had in weeks and a jam doughnut. It had occurred to her that she hadn't eaten all day and when she saw the doughnut in the cake stand on the counter waving at her she had to have it. The lady that served her was very pretty and far too well dressed to be working in a café. Lisa pictured her more as an air hostess or lady in a perfume shop.

She could see a grumpy greasy-haired looking woman sat near the window reading a magazine and constantly looking at her watch and occasionally scowling at the lady behind the counter. She looked like the sort of woman who rarely got five minutes to herself and was clearly agitated.

There were a couple of young mums with their pushchairs having a bit of a gossip, she tried to hear what they were talking about but it was all about school and other mums and men generally, nothing about the girl that had been attacked.

She was debating giving up when the tinkle of the front door bell of the café went and she was delighted to see the screaming woman and the handsome man she had seen that morning at the hospital throwing the ginger-haired boy out. Note to self she must start learning names.

She was fairly sure they hadn't seen her this morning but just in case she shrunk down in her chair and opened the Daily Wobble which she had grabbed at the local shop and pretended to read.

She could tell there was some tension between the two of them. They sat at a table nearby with their coffees, not giving Lisa a second glance.

"It was always supposed to just be a bit of fun in secret and now it's not," the handsome man said to her as quietly as he could, looking round the room to check nobody was listening. "And now all this with Trace," he seemed to stop mid-sentence hoping for a response.

"My best friend is in the hospital on a life support machine and you have decided that now is the time to finish with me," she replied quietly, shaking her head, laughing in disbelief.

"Technically we aren't an item to finish, it was just a bit of fun," he said arrogantly. She looked gobsmacked.

"Just a bit if fun? I was there for you, I helped you when you needed a friend, before all your dirty little secrets came out and this is how you thank me." He looked nervous.

"We had an agreement 'Chelle," he said sternly. "I'm not the only one sat at this table with secrets," he said venomously. She seemed to ponder this for a moment, they both stared angrily at each other.

"I have to go get ready for Ponsonby's party," she said getting up from the table and storming out of the café. Lisa could swear she saw the flicker of a smile on her face as she left. Something told her that this was not all over.

She was startled when all of a sudden her phone rang in her handbag. It was her mum. She had to get back to the hospital now. For once her career would have to wait. There was most definitely a story or two here though.

As she rushed out of the café she came face to face with none other than Rose Nutter. Rose worked at her paper the Daily Wobble as an agony aunt. Although their paths never crossed professionally they were always polite to each other. Wonder what she's doing her, at least I'll be able to get some first-hand gossip, she thought to herself.

Albert and Rose sat on the edge of their tiny uncomfortable bed in their room at The Mad Cow staring at their little evidence board. The board was covered in letters, magazine clippings, photographs, scribbled notes from Albert on the back of napkins and heart shaped post-it notes where Rose had made notes. They sat there for some time trying to take it all in. Although they had their theories there was no hard evidence. Rose had very briefly given Lisa a rundown of the key events. Although Lisa knew more technical details from the police and hospital than Rose, Rose was able to help with a bit of local knowledge. Normally she wouldn't approve of such things but if it helped highlight Trace's case more and catch her attacker then so be it. Lisa was going to do her own research and had promised to keep Rose updated.

"That's it!" Rose suddenly exclaimed. "That can't be a coincidence. Albert I know who it is!" With that, she then got up from the bed and went into the bathroom and shut the door leaving Albert sat alone on the bed.

"What?" Albert said. "What you doing woman? Who is it then?" he said in disbelief that she had just left him hanging like that.

"Can't hear you properly Albert I'm in the shower, we've got Ponsonby's posh do to get ready for. I'll tell you in a minute," she shouted through the shower noise. "Think we should keep it from Trish until after the party though, don't want to ruin the night."

"Are you kidding me?" he said to himself shaking his head knowing his wife was laughing to herself on the other side of that door. "Couldn't tell her if I wanted to could I, if you won't bloody tell me." They both laughed.

Chapter 17

Albert and Rose accompanied Graham and Denise in the walk through the village to the big house on the hill, the home of Mr Ponsonby-Gables. Ever the one to show off he had been more than happy for the Nutters to attend the bash after Mary had fluttered her eyelashes at him in the pub.

Denise and Graham were bickering as politely as they could within company. Graham clearly thought the party was a bad idea and wanted to stay home and hide whereas Denise thought it the right opportunity to show their faces to the village. God knows how she'd react when she found out Graham's secret. Albert shuddered at the thought of being in the room when that day came. He was hoping to witness one of her amusing drunken stories though, which George had described.

Rose was wearing a white dress with red roses which she had packed 'just in case.' It was one of Albert's favourites, she looked absolutely beautiful in it. She had put a few soft curls in her long dark hair and had attached a little red flower clip which was much more subtle than the huge fruit-based hat that she had worn to the church just a few days before. Her sparkly eyes twinkled even more as she linked her arm in her husband's. Albert himself scrubbed up alright too. He was wearing a grey-silver suit with waistcoat, which he hated but, although a bit overweight he was still ruggedly handsome.

As they neared the big beautiful brown brick house, music and laughter could be heard from the gardens. Denise and Graham led them round the side of the building into the back garden. The word 'garden' should be used lightly here, it was more of a field. Mr Ponsonby-Gables had fields upon fields as his back garden, all green and lush with a few trees thrown in. He had erected a white marquee near the house, and lots of white tables and chairs were scattered around. There was a small band of musicians playing beautifully on the patio. There were lots of people milling about, some they recognised from the village and many that clearly weren't local judging by the 'ya's', 'daalings', 'gollys' and 'gee whizzes'. Must be Ponsonby's rich friends.

Rose could tell Albert was uncomfortable already, well that was until a young waiter with a tray full of Pimms and Gin and Tonics arrived to offer them a drink. They both took one of each gratefully, as did Denise and Graham before scowling at each other and wandering off in different directions. Even the waiter was snooty and lifted his nose as he walked away.

Trish and the reverend, George and Mary were sat at a table on the lawn. Mary caught sight of them and smiled and waved them over. Mary was immaculate as always, she was wearing a navy dress with white polka dots and a contrasting red belt. Trish also looked lovely. So far she had been 'the vicar's wife' and a bit tired but she had her hair in an 'up do' piled on her head and was wearing a summer yellow dress and lots of make-up unusually.

The reverend was dressed semi-casually in a light blue shirt with his collar and George for once was not, and I repeat, was not wearing a cardigan but a smart pinstripe suit. The group generally looked uncomfortable. Trish as if reading their minds leaned in and whispered to Rose.

"Mr Ponsonby-Gables is quite an unlikable sort of man as I'm sure you are aware and are probably wondering why we are all here when we can't actually stand him." Rose nodded and smiled slightly embarrassed. "You see for all his faults he gives us a very generous donation to the church and the things we support like the women's shelter and the local fete if we come to his party once a year and spread the word amongst his toff friends how great he is which is a small price to pay really." She winked at Rose and Albert who both laughed.

Looking round they noticed Joyce wheeling her mother into a crowd of old ladies. Hilda was all in black with a weird hat which looked like it was older than her, and had what looked like a bird in a nest on top. Joyce herself, like George had hung up the cardigan for the day and was wearing a beige ladies skirt suit and white blouse. She must have already had a few to drink, she rather loudly 'cooeee'd' the reverend who politely waved back, then, as he looked away she scowled at Trish and Mary.

The snooty waiter arrived at their table with the tray of Pimms and Gin and Tonics, remembering he had just let them have a drink he turned to walk away.

"Leave the tray," Albert said.

"Certainly, sir," he said rolling his eyes. Albert didn't care that he didn't really belong here. Free food and drink and he would still make sure he enjoyed himself.

The reverend's brother the dishy chemist was sat at a nearby table with 'Chelle who looked like she had been drinking way before the party, and a couple of other women that Rose thought she recognised from bitch and stitch, sorry knit and natter. As he caught Rose's eye he smiled that dashing smile and waved. Rose went bright red and waved back as did the rest of their table.

"Certainly one for the ladies my baby brother," the reverend joked. Albert rolled his eyes.

As the afternoon continued, they could see that most people were getting more drunk and more loud.

Ponsonby was grabbing the bum of literally every woman who went near the buffet, including Trish who looked like she might throw him a right hook but didn't want to cause a scene. Rose had sent Albert to get her food, although with all the small petite posh bottoms at the party he wouldn't grab hers anyway probably, although he was pretty drunk. The only one who seemed obviously not to mind was Denise who giggled rather raucously and called him a naughty boy very loudly looking over her shoulder to check that her husband could hear. He responded by going over to sit at the same table as Penny which made Denise's face red with rage and she stormed off somewhere into the house.

"I love this place," Albert laughed shaking his head, "you never know what's going to happen." Rose nodded in agreement. This village seemed to beat most of the scandals on their favourite soap 'Illicit Relations'. They hadn't seen any of it while they were in Upper Wobble but having recorded it, would have a marathon Illicit Relations session when they got home, they had already agreed.

As it began to get dark, people started going home, the band and the caterers were starting to pack up. They were preparing themselves to leave when Ponsonby staggered over to their table.

"Taking this party inside now chaps," he said slurring, "come join me in the drawing room." He slapped Rose's bottom and put an arm round Albert leading him into the house. He looked over his shoulder rather pleadingly at Rose as he was led off to, "did you know this house was built by my great great great great grandfather in the eighteenth century" blurb coming from Ponsonby's drunken mouth.

The Goodsouls, Mary and George all looked like they really wanted to go.

"Well maybe just one more," the reverend said, "rather than be rude. I think I'll have a coffee though, feeling a bit squiffy." He smiled and winked at Rose. He really was a kind man she thought.

The five of them followed Albert inside as did a few others from the village.

Once Rose had discovered which of the many rooms they were going into she excused herself to find the ladies.

"What do you mean no more?" an angry lady's voice could be heard from down the corridor. It was the opposite end to where the toilet was but Rose crept towards the voices anyway. As she neared she could make out the two voices clearly now. It was Graham and 'Chelle.

"You have bled me dry 'Chelle. I don't have any more money to give you," he said angrily.

"So you want your wife to find out your dirty little secret then?" she replied nonchalantly.

"Of course not. All I can do is plead to your better nature to not ruin my life. I've never done anything to you. Please 'Chelle I'm begging you," he pleaded.

"We had an agreement," she said sternly. "You pay me what I ask or I reveal all to The Mad Cow herself and you will be humiliated."

"I don't have any more money," he said quietly. "I'm struggling as it is. Please 'Chelle. I know you've had some tough times but I really don't deserve this."

"Don't deserve it?" she snapped "You, your psycho wife and that pervert son of yours don't deserve to be punished? Don't make me laugh." Rose was shocked by the venom in her voice. She had heard enough and for fear of being caught she quickly and quietly started walking back down the corridor.

After taking a tiddle in quite possibly the poshest toilet Rose had ever entered she made her way back towards the group. She could hear some whispering voices coming from the kitchen, sounded like a very drunk Ponsonby. Rose stood still and held her breath listening.

"We had a deal," he spat angrily. "Let me down and I'll destroy you," he said with a shocking tone of venom and headed towards the kitchen door armed with more wine. "Ah Mrs Nutter!" he exclaimed, complete change of character, spotting her as he came out of the kitchen. He put his arm round her and dragged her off to the drawing room before she could see who it was he was speaking to.

People were milling about and mingling, coming in and out of the room, going to the loo, she'd never be able to tell who he had just threatened.

Albert was swaying a little if Rose was honest, as was the Reverend Goodsoul. A few faces they recognised were dotted around the room. They could see Denise's sister Penny talking to the same woman that worked in the chemist she had brought with her to The Mad Cow, both of them laughing.

The dishy chemist, the Reverend Goodsoul's younger brother had a young blonde on his knee. Albert still couldn't see what the fuss was about.

Joyce wheeled her mother Hilda in, once again running over Trish's toes.

"How clumsy of me!" she exclaimed sarcastically.

"Don't be silly, Joyce, it was an accident, no harm done," the drunk reverend replied as she beamed at him, Trish scowling at her trying to hold her tongue.

Rose very quickly and quietly tried to relay to Albert the conversations she had heard in the hallway. They knew Graham was being blackmailed for his secret and now they knew it was 'Chelle. Nasty bit of work she turned out to be. Ponsonby up until now had seemed a harmless old perv but there was nothing harmless in his threats just now.

'Chelle appeared back in the room looking angry, heading straight for Ponsonby who was pouring the drinks and snatching one off him she whispered something to him and he smiled. The look on both their faces made Rose shudder. They were up to something.

Graham returned to the room shortly after, a large whisky in his hand. He looked very pale indeed as he joined his wife.

"Where have you been?" she said rather loudly. He replied quietly to which Denise said loudly, "No we are not going home! I'm enjoying myself." Embarrassing him. He looked sad but not surprised. Albert and Rose felt very sorry for him as he pleaded with her to leave the party.

"Nutters!" Ponsonby appeared out of nowhere, once again slapping Rose on the bottom and putting an arm round Albert. "Let me show you my slide collection," he said excitedly as the rest of the room let out a joint groan. Obviously this was a regular thing that everyone else in the room had experienced many times and were not thrilled about it.

Within minutes the lights in the room had been dimmed, a projector appeared and a young Ponsonby's face had emerged on the massive screen. The slides were basically a collection of Ponsonby's travels over the years. Some very expensive and exotic places, basically what he was doing was flaunting his wealth.

"Aah Egypt," he said showing a picture of him stood in front of a pyramid. "The women there absolutely throw themselves at you." He grinned, the women in the room shuddered.

"Now here's me in India, beautiful country. The peasants treat you like a God there. You would not believe what you can get for a hundred rupees." He laughed loudly, nudging and winking at Albert. He is really a revolting man, Rose and Albert thought.

"Ah here's one of me, 'Chelle and Trace at a bar not too far from here." The three of them were sat in what looked like a lounge cabaret bar with different coloured cocktails, with various parrots and things sticking out of them smiling at the camera. He flicked through a few like this of them gradually getting more and more drunk as he flicked through. "Anybody recognise it?" he said, various murmurings around the room of yes and no. "What about you Graham?" he said seriously. Graham shook his head and looked at the floor. "No? Are you sure?" Graham was again trying to get his wife to leave tugging her arm, again she was having none of it.

"It's a very special bar this one, has some brilliant cabaret, we love the drag queen there don't we 'Chelle?" he said smiling

"Oh yeah she's brilliant, he's brilliant, whatever." They both laughed, some of the room joined in. "Ooh here's one of her now," he exclaimed. The picture showed a drag act in a green sequined dress and huge blonde wig on the stage. "What was her name again 'Chelle?" he asked. "Wilma," she said laughing. "Wilma Ballsdrop." The rest of the room joined in the laughter. Albert and Rose looked at each other knowing what was coming next. "We had some banter with Wilma, she was very funny. Had a very distinct almost recognisable voice." A zoomed in shot of Wilma appeared on the screen. 'Chelle took over the presentation.

"Imagine our surprise when after the show we went to meet Wilma and congratulate her on a brilliant show and this was what we saw." The next photograph appeared of Wilma, without her wig looking angry. 'Chelle was laughing with her wig in her hand. There was no denying it.

As it slowly dawned on the people in the room that Wilma Ballsdrop and Graham, landlord of The Mad Cow, were one and the same, gasps surrounded the room. Graham had his head in his hands. Denise looked like she was in shock. The entire room turned to stare at Denise and Graham.

Poor Graham looked like he wanted the floor to open up and swallow him whole. After some time Denise began slowly walking towards the big screen, swaying slightly with the alcohol and not surprisingly her dress was tucked in her knickers at the back. She stood directly in front of the screen staring then turned back to her husband then back to the screen then back to her husband.

"Is this true?" she slurred. He remained silent. "Is this you?" Again he said nothing. "Is this you?" she shrieked making everyone in the room jump.

"Yes," he said quietly. The room gasped. Denise seemed like she was trying to form a sentence but was really lost for words. The entire room stared at her waiting for her to speak. "Are you?" she began "Are you?" Graham finished the sentence.

"Gay?" he said. The room swung their heads to look at Graham. Denise flinched and nodded.

"No," he said warmly heading towards his wife. "I'm not gay. I'm your husband and I love you. Wilma," he indicated the screen, "Wilma is a hobby. A friend almost. I've been dressing as Wilma on the stage since college when I needed to earn extra money." Denise fell into the nearest chair and picked up the nearest drink as she took this in. "I've kept her a secret as I knew how you would react." She looked at him wide eyed. "At home I can't get a bloody word in edgeways." The entire room except Denise nodded along with that, he had a point. "And I don't want to. In The Mad Cow you are the boss. On that stage Wilma is in charge. So I dress in women's clothing occasionally and tell jokes." He was on his knees now in front of her. "I'm good at it and I have a huge following and it pays well." She remained silent.

"It's true he is good at it," her sister Penny interjected. Denise looked at her. "You knew about this?" she said angrily.

"I saw him there a few years ago when I went there on a hen party. He really is funny. He begged me not to tell you."

Denise remained silent, staring into space open mouthed, with the odd hiccup.

"Please, Denise, say something," Graham said taking her hands.

"I knew there was something going on, knew you two had secrets. I thought you were having an affair," she said quietly. The room gasped again as they looked on. 'Chelle looked disappointed at Denise's level of calm. Clearly she had been hoping to see her throw things at him.

"What?" he said shocked.

"I thought you were having an affair," she repeated.

"How could you think that? I love you Denise, I would never do that to you. Penny has helped me with buying makeup and tights and things like that that I can't easily go and get myself." He half laughed. "That's all."

"I saw the make-up on your clothes, smelt the ladies perfume on you and the fact that you are always so vague as to where you've been." She laughed now. "All this time." Shaking her head. "So where is all this money you've earned then?"

"I have some put aside, not as much as I'd hoped. I've been being blackmailed for a long time now to keep this secret."

"What!" she shouted. "Not you?" she exclaimed looking at Penny who looked gobsmacked.

"No, it was me," 'Chelle interjected arrogantly, another gasp from the room, "and tonight Graham told me he wasn't going to pay me anymore and I told him that he'd regret it." She looked at him venomously. Denise looked angry.

Whisperings and shaking of the head in disapproval began to emerge round the room. 'Chelle arrogantly walked over to the mini bar pouring herself a large drink.

"What?" she said when she realised the whole room was staring at her. Even Ponsonby looked taken aback, he must not have been aware of the blackmail either. "Oh come on, he's clearly a weirdo, know where that pervert son of his gets it from now. Caught him with Trace's knickers more than once, little thief," she laughed. Nobody in the room laughed with her. Denise stood up and walked over to her, staggering.

"What did you just say about my family?" she said angrily.

"Don't make me laugh Denise. You heard me just fine," she said. With that Denise grabbed a tray of vol au vents off the table nearby, rammed it into 'Chelle's body getting prawns and tuna and allsorts all over her dress and threw a glass of whisky right in her face to wash it down. Albert thought it was one of the funniest things he had ever seen. The room became a mixture of more gasping, gobsmacked laughter and cheering.

"You all think you are so perfect!" 'Chelle spat at the crowd wiping her face with a napkin. The room became silent. "The Mad Cow, the Cross Dresser and their Pervert Son," she said waving, gesturing towards Denise and Graham. "Your weird sister," she said waving at Penny. "Penny's pig awful pies, you thought she was having an affair, well she is," she laughed, "with Donna from the Chemist" The room gasped and turned to look at Penny and her lady friend Donna who were sat rather closely, instantly separating with shock. "And you two," she said pointing at Mary and George. "Mary and Ja Ja Ja George. Clearly he's old enough to be your dad, what's that about? Got Daddy issues have you Mary?" she said rudely. The room remained gobsmacked as she continued her outburst. "And Joyce seriously you are never going to get laid looking like that," she laughed. "What is it with you and cardigans? And how is your mother not dead yet? She must be at least a hundred and fifty by now, miserable as sin and deaf as a post." Joyce looked appalled, her mother Hilda hard of hearing could be heard whispering to Joyce, "What did she say?" Joyce didn't reply.

"Alright 'Chelle, think you've had enough," Jacob, the dishy chemist had removed the blonde from his knee and stood up. "Let me walk you home," he said kindly, taking her arm.

"Get off me!" she shouted "You don't want to me to even start talking about you! You might have some sort of power over half the women in this village but you do not control me." Her tone was venomous. He didn't push her on it.

"Now that's enough 'Chelle." Ponsonby suddenly intervened and attempted to lead her away. She shook him off.

"And you, you vile old pervert, nobody around here actually likes you, you know they just come for the free booze," she said sarcastically, toasting him with a champagne glass from the table before swigging it back in one.

"I say now that really is enough," the Reverend Goodsoul spoke up. "We understand you are going through a difficult time, 'Chelle, but this behaviour really is out of order." 'Chelle paused for a moment, Rose and Albert wondered if she was actually going to listen to him. After a short silence she began to laugh rather manically.

"What is so funny?" he said to her. "You have seriously hurt many people's feelings in the last few minutes and potentially ruined lives and marriages," he said angrily.

"What's so funny?" she said. "What's so funny? You are and that perfect wife of yours. She's the biggest liar in the room, at least I'm being honest."

"What do you mean?" he replied nervously.

"Come on, Reverend, you aren't daft, she's blatantly having an affair. Trace and I have seen her in town several times getting friendly with another bloke." The room gasped again. It's a wonder anyone in the room still had their breath what with all the gasping. The room span round to look at Trish.

"It's you!" Trish said angrily. "Sending the letters!" Trish said calmly standing up.

"What? What letters?"

"You know very well what letters," Trish replied loudly.

"I don't know what you are talking about," 'Chelle replied sounding rather bored.

"The hate mail letters," she said angrily.

Rose and Albert were about to intervene. They didn't have one hundred per cent proof but were almost certain they had discovered the culprit and were going to reveal all to Trish in the morning after the party. Surprisingly it wasn't 'Chelle.

"I don't know what you're talking about," 'Chelle said angrily.

"Well then who is it?" Trish said shouting now. So much for keeping it quiet and discreet. She had gone beyond that now and the champagne had given her a 'who cares about appearance' edge. "Which one of you is it?" she said to the room. "I know it's one of you here, I know it is." Nobody said a word. Trish was frantic now, the room staring at her as if she was mad. Rose and Albert looked at each other and nodded deciding to take a chance. Trish was looking rather insane at the moment and didn't need any more humiliation. The hate mailer was obviously too cowardly to speak up. Albert, seeing Trish wasn't getting anywhere whispered in Trish's ear.

"What?" she said quietly. "Are you sure?" he said to which he nodded.

The reverend who had remained quiet had sank into the nearest chair and grabbed a large whisky.

"Will someone please tell me what is going on here?" he said pleadingly.

"Are you going to tell him or shall I?" Trish said turning to Joyce. More shocked gasps from the room. Joyce's usually bland miserable face began laughing manically. Trish seemed to think about this for a moment unsure as to which would be worse then she sighed, resigning herself to the inevitability that this day would come eventually.

"I've been receiving some seriously cruel hate mail for some time now," she said to her husband.

"What? Gosh why didn't you say anything?" he responded. "We could have gone to the police," The reverend said then seeing his wife's face continued. "What was in these letters?"

"It is the nature of these letters that I did not want people knowing about, especially you." He looked puzzled. "They are full of secrets about my past, secrets that I didn't want anyone to know. Secrets of how I used to live my life and make money. I'm so sorry you had to find out like this Peter." She lowered her head in shame.

"It wasn't supposed to be like this. It was supposed to all be handled quietly. I enlisted the help of the Nutters here, they are private detectives," she said motioning to Albert and Rose who both smiled awkwardly. The rest of the room now knew why they were really there,

Rose went rather red in the face and had to nudge Albert as he went into his pocket about to start giving out business cards. "Time and place Albert," she muttered through gritted teeth.

"They were to help me find the hate mailer quietly in the hope that I could reason with them but clearly it's too late for that," Trish said looking angrily at Joyce's smug face.

"It was me, Reverend," Joyce said proudly. "She deceived you and I wanted you to know the truth. I learnt of her sordid past even before Maud was dead."

"Oh my God," Trish said slowly putting a hand to her mouth as if something had dawned on her. "Ida," she said. "You spoke to Ida." Joyce smiled smugly.

"Who's Ida?" the reverend spoke

"Ida was evil," Trish answered. "She was the woman who talked me into that life. Made me think I was worthless and had no other option. She's the woman that killed my best friend, Amelia. I don't know how but I know that she did," Trish said angrily. "Imagine my shock when I saw her again all those years later on the same ward as Maud." Trish took over. "I did my best to have nothing to do with her. The fact I had to care at all for that evil woman was too much to bear." Joyce decided to interrupt.

"We were visiting Maud when she came in and I saw your reaction when you laid eyes on her. Knew there was something not right." Trish sank into a chair, unable to stand much longer.

"I noticed nobody visited her so when we went to visit Maud I started talking to her. Seemed we shared a mutual interest or should I say hatred. You." The room remained silent. "She told me everything, all about the whore you used to be," Joyce spat. Trish flinched at the word and the rest of the room gasped. "Did you know that, Reverend? That your perfect Patricia used to be a low class and from what I hear low price prostitute!" She continued scathingly. The reverend remained silent from the shock. He was looking at his wife who couldn't bear to look back at him.

Joyce went over to him and knelt beside him. "I could make you so happy, Reverend," she said smiling. "Not only is it what Maud would have wanted it, but I am not dirty and used like this one." She pointed at Trish. "I am pure," she said proudly, a manic gleam in her eyes.

"No surprise there," Albert muttered to Rose who half smiled as she elbowed him in the ribs to be quiet. George was sat beside the reverend. The reverend turned to look at him and decided to take the large glass of whisky from George's hands and drink it all in one.

"My love," Joyce said. "Shall I get you another?" He nodded, still with a face of shock. Joyce rushed to the first glass of whisky she saw, this one had just been poured by Ponsonby for himself and he was about to take a sip before she snatched it. The reverend again drank this one down in one. "I would bring you drinks every day, and meals, well I'm a marvellous cook as you know, we would be so happy." The whole room seemed to take a deep breath at the same time. Trish was looking at the ground as if she knew this day would come eventually. Joyce was still talking rubbish about how happy she would make him when he finally spoke.

"Joyce," he said quietly.

"Yes my darling?"

"Will you just shut up!" he shouted. The entire room jumped including Trish. I don't think any of them had ever heard the reverend shout before. "I don't care what Trish did in her past. Everyone has a past. You really think I'm just going to forget that I'm in love with my wife and run off into the sunset with you and dragging along your mother," indicating Hilda who seemed flabbergasted. "Who might I add is one of the most unpleasant women I have ever met." The room gasped again "And you think this is what Maud would have wanted! Maud couldn't stand you, she just tolerated you because she was kind, much like Trish does now. You need help Joyce, professional help." With that he took Trish's hands. She stood up as if in a daze. She had not expected any reaction like this at all. "Now if you'll all forgive me, I'm going home to sleep with my wife," he said and kissed her

174

passionately. "Let's go home darling," Albert, Rose, Mary and George couldn't hide the glee from their faces, Ponsonby yelled "Hear hear" and raised his glass in a drunken toast as they all watched the Goodsouls walk towards the door. "Oh and your services are no longer required at the vicarage," the reverend said. "My wife is more than capable. Such cruel behaviour," he said sadly shaking his head. "May God forgive you."

*

The man sat in his car, watching the interfering whore and the reverend staggering home giggling through the village like teenagers. They disgusted him. Their happiness would be short lived though. He would get his revenge.

*

Albert and Rose were once again strolling arm in arm through the village square. It was late morning and they would be leaving Upper Wobble later that day now that the mystery of Trish's hate mailer had been solved. Well I say solved, more of an educated guess they both joked. It was their first real case after all. Sadly it had not been solved quietly and discreetly as Trish had hoped, 'Chelle and Joyce had made sure of that. The Reverend Goodsoul's reaction however had taken Trish by surprise. He didn't give a damn about her past. He had been no angel before he had found God. They had both saved each other and he loved her even more. Also he had asked Joyce never to return to their home for her deception and cruel behaviour towards his wife which had made Trish extra happy.

They were just nearing the edge of the square when they saw Mary storming towards the church, George was a few feet behind her huffing and puffing to keep up, getting rather red-faced in a pale lemon and navy diamond cardigan.

"What's wrong?" Rose asked as Mary neared them.

"It's Trish and the reverend," Mary said barely slowing down and sounding frantic. "They are missing."

Chapter 18

The Nutters followed Mary and George up the path to the door of the vicarage.

"I've got a bad feeling about this," she had said. Trish was at home but the house was in almost complete blackness. "I haven't heard from either of them all morning, neither of them is answering their phone. We were supposed to be meeting with the village fete committee at the community centre but they never showed, it's so unlike them." Mary sounded very worried.

"Are you sure they aren't just getting reacquainted if you know what I mean?" Albert joked but as they neared the house they could see that the curtains of the house were all drawn and plant pots and garden ornaments near the front door had fallen over and were mashed.

Albert managed to peer through the window round a small gap at the curtain edge. The house was dark but he could see signs of a struggle, there were photographs smashed, a tall lamp had been knocked over.

"We need to call the police," he said calmly.

"There's no time!" Mary shouted, she was sifting through the plant pots looking for the spare key when they heard a scream from behind them. It was coming from the church. "That sounded like Trish," she said, taking off towards the church, even in her red stilettos she was very quick.

Albert and Rose followed as quickly as they could, puffing and panting after her and George likewise behind them. Mary indicated to them to be quiet and the four of them snuck into the church.

Inside the church lobby the crowd could see through the glass doors straight down the church aisle. Trish and the Reverend Goodsoul appeared to be tied back to back on chairs besides the altar. Both of them looked bloodied and bruised. A large man probably in his fifties was walking up and down with a noticeable limp. He was talking to them angrily.

"Oh Patricia, Patricia," the man laughed loudly. "When I saw your face on that notice board, 'Vicar's Wife organises successful local Charity event' well I nearly cried with laughter. It was like a sign from God wasn't it, Vic?" he laughed some more shoving the Reverend Goodsoul who remained silent.

"Am I going to hell, Reverend?" he laughed manically. The reverend remained silent. "I didn't intend to kill a vicar when I was fantasising about killing your wife over breakfast this morning but you insisted on being in the wrong place at the wrong time and then were foolish enough to try and stop me," he laughed insinuating that nothing or no one could stop him. "If all sinners go to hell then your perfect little whore of a wife here is coming with me." He had a large kitchen knife in his hand which he stroked along Trish's cheek. She flinched at his touch but remained calm.

"I've been looking for your wife for a long time, Reverend. Admittedly I didn't know it was her I wanted, no-one can replace my Amelia but her interfering got my wife killed and now she'll have to pay," he said venomously before continuing. "I nearly fell over when I heard that she had become a vicar's wife" he laughed some more.

"What do you want with us?" the reverend spoke quietly. Ivan thought for a minute.

"Well I didn't want anything with you but seeing as you insisted on trying to protect your wife it looks like I'll have to kill you both now doesn't it?" he shouted in the reverend's face.

"You don't need to do this, Ivan," Trish said shaking her head.

"Oh but I do. You interfered in my marriage, tried to take my wife away from me, my Amelia, who I paid for fair and square by the way," he said as an aside. "I was forced to kill my Amelia to make sure she could never leave me." He laughed at the irony. "It felt so good killing her you know, I didn't even mind having to clean up the blood"

"I knew you'd killed her, knew you would eventually. I begged her to get away from you but she wouldn't listen, she was so scared, scared you'd find her." He smiled at this, almost like it was praise. "What did you do to her?" she pleaded. He leaned down close to her ear

"I threw her out like the trash she was," he spat. Albert thought he saw a flicker of a smile cross Trish's face. He had sent Rose outside to call the police. He knew he would have to intervene if the police didn't hurry up but right now while this mad man was busy talking and loving the sound of his own voice he was prepared to let him get on with it. George and Mary at his side remained silent.

"Do you know," he said rather conversationally, "this is the exact same knife I used on her." He was admiring the knife, twirling it in his hands. "There is something you can do for me," he said. Walking over to a holdall on the floor he pulled out a red wig, the perfect shade of Amelia's hair. "You are sick," Trish said as he shoved it roughly on her head as she struggled. Finally she gave up struggling; he stared at her admiringly on his knees in front of her. He stroked the wig. He returned to the holdall and pulled out a pair of bloodied slippers. Trish kicked out as he fought to put them on her feet.

"Please don't hurt my wife," the reverend pleaded with him. "I don't care about her past, I can't lose my wife, not again," he sobbed. Trish began to cry too, their hands were tied behind their backs but Trish was able to grasp her husband's fingers.

"Enough!" the man shouted in such an angry loud voice, making them all jump. "It is time," he said. Smiling at Trish he raised his knife.

*

December 1988

Amelia gingerly stepped out of the bath. The water had been scorching hot but she couldn't feel it any more. She

178

couldn't feel much of anything anymore. She was dead inside. Numb. Had been for some time.

For a moment recently she had felt something, he had made her feel again, feel beautiful and worth something but then her husband had found her, like he always did. That's why running was pointless.

She stood in front of the bathroom mirror. It was covered with condensation from the heat of the bath. She groaned as she stretched up to wipe it with her fingers. She stared at the face in the mirror, a face she barely recognised. The bruises and cuts were still raw and so sore. How had this happened? How had she become this? Trish her one friend had tried so hard to help her but she just pushed her away. She had tried the police before and nothing had happened, he could talk his way out of anything. She was too frightened to try again after the beating she had last time. Besides what would she do without him? Where would she live?

She laughed at the irony of preferring to go back to that house, that house where it all started, than living here in this beautiful little cottage. This idyllic country cottage with its evil and secrets.

She opened the cupboard and grabbed the painkillers. It was not the first time she had considered taking the lot. Maybe today would be the day, the day it would all be over. She poured them into her hand and stared at them a while almost in a trance. She jolted out of it to the sound of the doorbell downstairs. Who on earth was that? Her husband was at work so obviously couldn't answer it. She put the tablets back in the bottle quickly and gingerly stepped down the stairs.

"Amelia? Are you there?" a kind voice spoke through the letter box. "It's me. I waited for him to leave for work, I know you are in there," she said sadly. "Please let me help you. I know you asked me not to come but I'm not giving up on you yet."

A tear fell down Amelia's cheek. She didn't even try to wipe it away, it burned hot, she could feel it. She stepped down the last step, tied her gown tightly round her waist and opened the door slowly to her one and only friend, who gasped!

*

Present

Albert saw the maniacal glint in the man's eye. He had seen it before, the last time on the face of the clown that had ended his police career. This man knew what he was doing and would not stop until he was caught.

Rose was back by his side and the police were on their way but there was no time. He looked at her face and knew she understood. He kissed her on the forehead and prepared himself to open the door, walk down the church aisle and confront this nutter, pardon the expression. Before he could though, something suddenly flipped in Mary. She had seen her friend hurt enough, opened her floral handbag, and with her beautifully manicured nails took out a gun. She walked slowly and carefully down the aisle towards the evil man and his prisoners. Albert, Rose and George had followed initially trying to stop her.

"I'll deal with this," she said in such a way that they all knew not to argue. She was holding the gun very steadily pointing it at the man's head. The man saw Trish and the reverend looking behind him shocked and spun round. When his eyes took in the beautiful blonde woman that stood before him he froze on the spot like he had just seen a ghost.

*

January 1989

"Miss?" A kind voice spoke from behind her. She remained silent. "Miss? Are you alright?" She still didn't respond. She couldn't get the words out. She turned to face the man. He had kind eyes and he smiled at her knowingly. "Come on," he said taking off his coat and putting it round her shoulders. "Let's get you inside in the warm." He led her slowly towards the front door of the large house. Her friend *had told her about it, somewhere where she could run to and be looked after.*

She didn't know how long she had been stood outside trying to pluck up the courage to go in. She was so numb with cold but she didn't care. This kind gentle man led her towards the door which opened before they reached it. It was her friend Trish. She hugged her tightly and let the tears flow.

"I'll put the kettle on," the kind man said.

"That would be lovely thank you, George" Trish replied.

February 1989

Amelia's heart was pounding. She knew Ivan would be home any minute. It was a Friday. He always went to the pub after work on a Friday, drank as much as he could fit in and then actually got in his car and drove home around eight o'clock. How he had never killed anyone she would never know.

He had steak on a Friday, rare and bloody. God help her if she overcooked it. Tonight however he would get a bit more than he bargained for with his steak. Providing she had the nerve to see it through. Her hands were shaking. She put down the brown-handled kitchen knife, had a large sip of wine and took some deep breaths. She pulled the pill bottle from her apron, began opening the tablets and collecting the contents. When she had enough she tipped them into a brand new bottle of whisky and replaced the lid, shaking the bottle until the white powder had fully dissolved. Then she poured her husband a very large glass.

*

When it was done she called her friends. Trish and George had been upstairs hiding in a cupboard in the spare room, supplies at the ready. They crept quietly down the stairs where Amelia was sat at the dining table drinking her wine. Ivan's head was slumped on his chest. He was clearly out cold.

"We'll never get away with this," Amelia said quietly shaking her head. "He'll know, he'll find me. He always does."

George went over to her and knelt beside her. Taking her hands in his he spoke clearly and sincerely and without a stutter.

"Not this time my love. Your pain, all of this, ends tonight. Tomorrow we start our new lives, away from here, in our quiet little village. I promise to love and look after you for the rest of my life. This man will not touch you again."

"When he comes round," Trish said, "he won't try looking for you. He will know that you are dead because he killed you." She smiled and pulled the bag of blood from her rucksack.

Amelia looked at them both. Her two best friends. She loved them both. If this worked she would be forever in their debt. She glugged back the last of her wine and smiled. The first real smile that she had smiled in years. "Ok," she said, "let's do this."

*

When they were finished the place looked like there had been a massacre. They had smashed plates and overturned the coffee table, knocked over ornaments to make it look like there had been a struggle. The three of them carried Ivan to the sofa and placed the blood-smeared knife in his pocket.

Amelia poured the whisky away and placed a half drunk bottle beside him on the floor. They remembered to put some blood in the car boot along with the clump of hair Amelia had willingly pulled from her own head and one of her slippers. The other was left in the hallway, blood smeared. When they were content that they had done all they could, George rolled up the rug in the hallway and the three friends walked out the front door.

Amelia was dead.

*

Amelia had fallen asleep in the car. George and Trish didn't want to wake her. Trish opened the front door of George's cottage quietly as George carried her inside. He carried her upstairs and placed her gently on the bed. She opened her eyes gently and smiled at him. He suddenly became very nervous.

"Sorry, we tried not to wake you," he said apologetically. "I I I have brought you some new clothes, in the wardrobe and drawers there." He pointed nervously. "With Trish's help of course," he smiled. "And and and there is a new toothbrush and things in the bathroom, just down the corridor. Anything else you need please let me know and I'll go shopping first thing."

Amelia took in her surroundings. The bedroom in George's cottage was cosier than she could have imagined. The bed clothes were a warm sunshine yellow and the bed itself so soft. For the first time in a long time she felt safe. He walked over to her, brushed the hair from her face and kissed her forehead. "Please try and get some sleep my love," he said as he walked towards the bedroom door.

"George," she said quietly. He turned to her, she was holding a hand out to him. "I don't know how I can ever thank you for this. She began to sob quietly, the first tears she had cried in a long time. Tears of relief and joy. They lay on top of the bed in an embrace and stayed that way until the sun came up.

*

Present

"But you're dead," the man said in disbelief. "I killed you," he continued, angrily brandishing the knife.

"No sweetheart," she said sarcastically. "I just let you think that you did." She smiled at him. His face had turned red with anger.

"No." He shook his head. "I killed you." He walked slowly towards her. "I took this very knife and slit your throat," he said sinisterly. Mary was still smiling at him. This seemed to make him even angrier.

"Don't be silly darling," she said very sarcastically. "How on earth would I be stood here now if you had killed me?" She laughed at him. She recounted in great detail the events of that night as both the man, Rose and Albert listened shocked and open mouthed at her tale. Rose and Albert couldn't help but smile as she smiled, at the brilliance of it.

As the truth began to dawn on Ivan that the words she was saying were actually the truth the anger in him at the humiliation took over and he lunged at Mary taking her completely by surprise. She fell backwards the gun going off in her hand shattering the stained glass window behind Trish and the reverend who were showered with glass.

Ivan was on top of her, the knife still in his hand trying to stab her throat. She was strong now though. Much stronger than he would ever have imagined she could be. She held his wrists tightly with both her hands outstretched above her, he pushing his weight down as she held him off as hard as she could. Albert and George together ran down the aisle towards them, George getting their first, surprisingly quickly for an older guy, Albert and Rose both noted, even though due to recent evens he had massively gone up in their estimation. George pounced on Ivan sending him to the ground his hands round his throat.

"You may have killed your Amelia but you will never kill my Mary," he said to Ivan with venom. Ivan still had hold of the brown-handled kitchen knife and was just able to swipe it at George cutting him deeply as Albert kicked it out of his hands. George screamed in pain and let go of Ivan who scrambled to his feet quickly as if to take off. Albert tackled him fiercely by the ankles (he had played rugby at school, you know) both men crashing to the floor. Ivan kicked out viciously kicking Albert in the face, his nose bleeding profusely. Ivan began to run down the aisle with his limp prominent towards the door.

Rose absolutely furious at her husband's bloodied nose without thinking launched her huge handbag (which weighed a tonne as it literally contained everything except the kitchen sink) at Ivan's head smashing him in the face and knocking him sideways into a pew (they said afterwards if it hadn't been a life or death situation it would have been one of the funniest things they had ever seen).

He stumbled back up to his feet and continued on his escape route just reaching the door when a shot was fired into the air stopping him in his tracks. He turned, this time placing his arms above his head in surrender.

"Amelia don't be stupid," he said to her patronisingly.

"My name is Mary," she said calmly.

"Whatever, just put the gun down for God's sake." She seemed to think about this for a moment, she was no murderer after all and hearing the sirens nearby began to lower the gun. He smirked at her.

"Huh," he said arrogantly. "Still doing what you are told," he laughed. "You never did have any guts," he sneered at her and with that Mary raised the gun and with a very steady hand and not an ounce of remorse she pulled the trigger.

Chapter 19

Mary was right. She wasn't able to kill anybody. She had shot Ivan in the leg and he had been taken away by ambulance with a police escort. Other paramedics had taken care of Albert and George's cuts and scrapes but they were all going to be fine.

Scottie had been about to arrest Ivan when DI Plonker pushed in to take the glory as he always did. He had almost arrested George first mind you after seeing that the other man had been shot he must instantly be the victim. Albert had a few choice words for him as you can imagine.

Mary or Amelia may have to face charges with relation to illegal possession of a firearm but they all agreed the shooting was in self-defence and either way, to Mary, totally worth it.

The Nutters, Mary, George, Trish and the reverend were assembled in The Mad Cow. Denise had again been very quick to get the brandy out to calm all their nerves and be the first to get all the gossip of course.

The tension between Denise and her husband seemed to have waned somewhat. They were actually smiling and talking and Graham patted her bottom as he walked past her and she giggled. It seemed she was so relieved to hear that he wasn't having an affair with her sister but was instead a very famous member of the drag queen society. He had such a passion for it and was actually very funny she had to admit. He swore that he was not gay nor did he have any inklings in that direction but he loved dressing up as his alter ego 'Wilma Ballsdrop' and had secretly earned quite a lot of money from it.

After Ponsonby's eventful bash they had gone home and talked and talked into the wee hours, something they hadn't done properly in years. She had always suspected Graham had had an affair and had even suspected it had been her sister Penny.

Denise had bridges to build including the one with her sister but she was tired of fighting. Even Graham Jr seemed to be happier. He was speaking almost full sentences to people and had been seen smiling at customers. Ivan's arrest meant the village had begun speaking to him again, Trace's police guard had been removed and he could visit her again.

The group had been laughing and enjoying themselves, all of them somewhat relaxed when Scottie walked in in his police uniform.

"Scottie, come join us," Albert said putting an arm round him and leading him towards the group.

"Sorry Albert, still on duty," he said glumly.

"What's wrong?" Albert said reading his face. Normally after such a good arrest they would be celebrating but Scottie's demeanour was the opposite.

"Bad news I'm afraid," he said. "Ivan has confessed to all of the red head murders. Eleven in total going back nearly twenty five years." Mary held her heart and burst into tears. She had felt terrible guilt, that her leaving Ivan all those years ago had turned him into this monster, that somehow it was all her fault. To hear he had been doing this since before she came along was both a shock and a relief."

"So what's the problem then?" Albert asked.

"He confessed to all but one. Trace."

"What?!" they all said in unison.

"He says he had nothing to do with it."

"That can't be right," Mary said. It fits with the others, same style, this village. It must be him." The rest of the group murmured in agreement.

"At first we thought he was just playing us up but he's right. The night Trace got attacked he was thirty miles away beating a young runaway to death with a hammer."

Chapter 20

The village of Upper Wobble didn't sleep well at all that night. When they thought Trace's attacker had been caught they had all breathed a huge sigh of relief. To know that it was an outsider, not one of their own, was the most important thing. But now after this revelation they began looking suspiciously at each other again.

Albert had an idea, it might not work but with a bit of co-operation, persuasion and telling a few porkie pies here and there, there was every chance it would.

The Reverend Goodsoul had called a meeting at the church hall for the village, for them all to air their views and in turn have a bit of a question and answer session with the Police.

Tonker stood at the front of the hall, trying to push his chest out like a peacock over his not very well hidden beer belly. Smythe stood next to him with a clipboard and pen doing his very best to look official. Rose and Albert sat towards the back; Rose nodded to Lisa Von-Winkleknicker who was hearing everything and writing down frantically in her notebook.

'Chelle was sat near the front with Ponsonby (who looked very bored by the whole thing) and a few other friends, including Mr Dishy Chemist (Albert had forgotten his actual name by now) and some other friends of theirs. They had all glared at Graham, Denise and Graham Jr who sat quietly towards the back on their way in.

Joyce was there too with her mother Hilda, who she once again had to repeat everything for. She had agreed to counselling and Hilda had agreed to some home help so that Joyce could have a bit of a life of her own and find some sanity hopefully. Maybe even a fella? Stranger things had happened. That had been the deal for Trish and the reverend to not take police action against her. Despite everything they still had a huge capacity for compassion.

The room was a hubbub of noise and comments and shouting and nobody could get a word in edgeways.

"What do you mean Trace's attacker is still out there!" someone shouted from the crowd. This was followed by lots of helpful comments such as:

"Why haven't you arrested him yet?"

"But you've got the mad man in custody!"

"Well it must be him no-one from our village would do such a thing."

"He must have done both, you must have your timings wrong."

"Bloody police are useless," and so on and so forth.

Finally the Reverend Goodsoul spoke up in quite the booming voice. Obviously used to public speaking he managed to quiet them all down so Tonker could speak.

"Now if you'll all just listen to what Inspector Plonker, sorry Tonker has to say ladies and gentleman." Albert sniggered, Plonker rolled his eyes.

"The man we arrested was not responsible for the attack on Trace. We have evidence to prove that that is the case. I'm sorry to have to tell you this but Trace's attacker is still out there." The crowd began jeering again, the reverend shushed them as best he could.

"I'm sure you are all quite safe and that Trace's attack was a youth mugging that got out of hand and was an isolated incident, not some mad serial killer. Trace is recovering well and the doctors have informed us that she will have a nice peaceful rest tonight then tomorrow they will be bringing her out of the coma and we will all see how much she can remember."

"What if she can't remember?" someone from the crowd shouted.

"Up until now they thought she might not remember anything but scans have shown that her brain is healing very well and she should remember everything in time. As soon as she tells us who it was we will of course arrest them." The room erupted into conversation once more.

Lisa Von-Winkleknicker sat at the hospital besides her Grampy's bed once more. The phone call from her mum had frightened her and prepared her for the worst but here he was days later, still fighting. She had taken pages of notes during her very brief stint in Upper Wobble and had also done some serious Googling of the locals. The inspector didn't even seem convinced that it was just a mugging gone wrong even though that was what he tried to convince the village this evening. He may be right. She had her own ideas though.

The ginger-haired boy who she knew had been prime suspect seemed genuinely too upset. He was odd, his mother was in fact a Mad Cow and she had heard from Rose how his dad had been revealed as local drag act Wilma Ballsdrop. They were one messed up family according to gossip.

Mr Ponsonby-Gables. She had lots of hits when she put his name into Google. The village seemed to be very nice to a man with lots of money even though he had been arrested for beating his first wife, she had discovered. Not convicted. She had dropped the charges and taken a fat cash settlement and a divorce instead. Wonder if the village knew all that?

Trace's best friend 'Chelle too had been in and out the courts and the papers more than once, especially in her youth. Various minor assaults and vandalism charges. Usually alcohol involved but nonetheless she had form on paper.

Still if they were bringing Trace out of her coma tomorrow then she hopefully would give them all the answers. Lisa would make sure she was there to get the scoop. In fact it was pretty quiet here at the moment, she might take a wander over there now.

He crept quietly down the corridor. His soft-soled shoes barely made a sound. Hospitals were scary places at night. He smiled, ironically the only thing he had to fear was Trace waking up and telling all. He wasn't even sure if she knew it was him or not but his reputation meant too much to risk it.

The ward was eerily quiet, all the patients were asleep and there was just one nurse on the desk. She smiled at him kindly, recognising him from previous visits, commenting on the huge bunch of flowers he was carrying. The unusual hour made no difference in the intensive care ward. They understood that potentially time with patients here was precious so were fairly lenient. Besides he had been clever, he had visited her late before. 'Work commitments' he thought he had said, so he knew that he wouldn't look out of place tonight. He knew that her police guard was being lifted today, waste of man power so knew he would be safe tonight. He entered the room quietly closing the door behind him. He placed the flowers at her bedside with the others and stroked her long red hair. He spoke aloud to her.

"Oh Trace," he sighed. "I'm sorry it had to come to this. I'm a very proud man and you." He paused. "You rejected me," he said calmly. "As if you had the right." He shook his head in disbelief. "I can have anyone I want and you had the nerve to turn me down." He sounded angry now. "This is your own fault you know," he continued very matter of fact. "I'll accept you weren't quite the air head I had you down as but to say you'd rather have that weedy little scrote from the pub than me, well that was just insane." He sounded disgusted. She looked so peaceful, he thought to himself. Well soon she would be at peace. He reached into his pocket and took out the syringe.

Albert hit the light switch illuminating the creepy scene in front of him. The man spun round in shock, syringe in his hand glinting in the light. The man went to run for the door and came face to face with Plonker, Smythe and Scottie. Knowing that he had been set up and that there was no way out he dropped the syringe and put his hands in the air. Mr perfect wasn't so perfect after all, Albert thought to himself.

Lisa Von-Winkleknicker had once again come round the corner at the exact right moment, her jaw dropped as she saw the police leading the terribly handsome young chemist chap from Trace's room in handcuffs. She immediately grabbed her phone and started taking pictures. She would get her scoop finally.

Chapter 21

In the days surrounding the arrest of "The Dishy Chemist / Reverend's Brother" the village of Upper Wobble was in complete shock.

The man that was entrusted with all their lives on a daily basis was also a narcissistic attempted murderer and as it happened, stealing and dealing prescription medication from the pharmacy.

The Reverend Goodsoul had taken it very hard indeed but his parish and his wife were behind him and they all needed each other at a time like this, he told his parishioners the next Sunday. He had been expecting an empty church but had in fact the complete opposite and was very moved by the support.

Trace, as predicted all along was taken out of her coma the following day and as it happened she remembered everything.

She like all the girls in the village had been infatuated with him and when he had asked her out she couldn't believe her luck.

"I wasn't surprised that he wanted to keep our first date secret," she said speaking to the room from her hospital bed. Her gentle voice had a distinct Essex girl tone to it but was very sincere. "Half the village fancy him and the rest love to gossip about him. He was late to The Giddy Boat and I thought he wasn't coming but then he turned up and straight away wanted to go somewhere else which at the time I didn't think strange just went with it," she continued.

"Where did you go?" Rose asked her.

"Well for a while nowhere really, just drove around. He said he wanted to take me back to his to show me something but wanted to wait until it was dark and late so they wouldn't be seen. I've known him since I moved to this village but never been alone with him or had a proper conversation with him, just admired those big blue eyes from afar like everyone else has. What I realised when talking to him though, the more and more he spoke I just thought to myself 'what a plonker'," she said with disbelief. "No offence, Inspector," she said to Tonker.

"My name is Tonker," he corrected her sharply. She ignored this and continued.

"So anyway I had of course known for some time how Gray felt about me," she said, (Gray was her name for Graham Jr, as she squeezed his hand.) He had been the first one at her bedside when she awoke. "'Chelle and that all made it out like he was some sort of stalker but he really wasn't. He is one of the loveliest kindest gentlest men I have ever met, just took a date with a madman for me to realise it." She smiled at him sheepishly. "Anyway I found myself all the while Jacob was talking to me thinking how I'd rather be at the kennels with 'Gray' walking and playing with the homeless dogs, that's how we met you see." She blushed. The Nutters had learnt this from Denise earlier of course.

"I tried to make some excuses and hint to him that I was tired and he just kept taking that to mean I was coming on to him like!" she said showing her shock. "Even when we got back to the village and I tried to go home he thought I was playing hard to get and tried to get physical with me. I got away and shrugged him off, I'm used to my share of creeps so I wasn't frightened particularly, just annoyed. Something in his face changed though and he became angry rather than playful. He couldn't believe that I wasn't interested, acted like there was something wrong with me! I made some comment about him being a creep and he said something about "'Chelle didn't think so" which made me mad. I wasn't surprised 'Chelle had been sleeping with him just disappointed cos he was such a plonker as it turned out."

'Chelle was stood towards the back of the room staring out of the window. She looked truly ashamed that she had fallen for such a man. It was 'Chelle that had informed the police about him selling prescription drugs. Somehow he had been fiddling the books at the chemist because he had a huge stash of various pills and cash under his bed. He was up to his eyeballs in debt and had talked Ponsonby into being one of his biggest clients. Trace continued. "Then he made a snide comment about Gray, knowing we were close and I slapped him right across the face I did!" she seemed rather proud of herself at this point, Albert and Rose also were proud of her. "I turned to walk away from him, heading towards home and the next thing I know 'Whack'! and I'm on the ground. The pain hurt so much I just closed my eyes and it all went black. Next thing I know I'm waking up here in this hospital bed." They all had to admire her, she knew how to tell a story.

"I was sure Amelia was dead," Trish said. "Women went missing all the time from that house for various reasons. I'd heard rumours that some were even sold," she said disgusted. The Nutters were seated in the same floral sitting room at the vicarage they had met George, Mary, Trish and the reverend in. They had been invited back for an afternoon tea as they all wanted to thank them personally – and of course give them their cheque.

"I used to see her or thought I did in town. I'd call after women in the street who looked like her, they all must have thought I was mad," she laughed sadly. "Then one day, years later, I was sitting in a café in town and a woman walked past, a woman with red hair. By this stage I had given up running after people and accepted that she was gone so I just looked away. Then something happened inside me. I just had a feeling that it was her.

"I ran out of the café leaving my bag and coat and everything behind and went after her. I called her name as I had done a million times before but this time the woman stopped. Stopped and turned to me. I could see the recognition in her face, along with a faint bruise she had tried to hide with make-up.

I had worked at the shelter for several years by this stage so saw that look too often." She looked at her friend kindly. Albert and Rose couldn't believe that Mary, this strong powerful beautiful woman had once been an abused housewife.

"I took her back to the café and we talked. Not for very long as she had to get home to Ivan. If she was late he would be very angry and very suspicious, but we met regularly after that.

"I learnt that she had been bought by Ivan from Ida and kept in a basement for some time. Eventually he let her out and classic Stockholm syndrome she was eventually allowed to go shopping by herself and still always went home to him. To have that level of control over her, she had had many many years of abuse."

"I couldn't leave him," Mary said. "He had me thinking that life without him would have been worse and that wherever I went he would find me and I believed him." She sighed. "He gave me a nice home and nice things which I had never had before, along with the bruises and the scars," she said angrily. "To think that all that time I was actually living with a murderer. I knew he'd kill me eventually if I didn't kill myself first," she said, "but I had no idea he was already a murderer." George, sitting quietly next to her held her hand. "Plucking up the courage to leave him was both the hardest and the easiest thing I ever had to do." She smiled at the irony. "I would never have done it without Trish and George though. I owe them my life," she said looking at them both with gratitude in her eyes.

Trish, Mary and George recounted that night again in even more detail to the Nutters. The night they had set Ivan up for Amelia's murder. They couldn't understand how he had just cleaned up and got on with it. They assumed he would go to the police in search of his missing wife and that when they investigated all the evidence would point straight at him and he'd go to prison.

"I even popped round a few times afterwards asking after her to keep up the pretence," Trish said. "He told me she had gone to stay with her mother for a while." Trish laughed "Obviously I knew from our days together in that house that she didn't have a mother. Eventually he became aggressive and threatened me so I didn't bother anymore."

"I didn't leave George's house in almost a year I was so frightened. I dyed my hair blonde almost immediately when I moved in with George. I knew Ivan was obsessed with my red curls. It was so long you see as he wouldn't allow me to get it cut. How mad is that?" she half laughed. The room became quiet for a while, contemplating all that they had heard.

"How did you realise it was Joyce sending the hate mail?" Trish asked the Nutters collectively. "I mean I knew she had a thing for Peter and disliked me thoroughly but to do that to me and then be able to come and work in my house." She shook her head in disbelief.

"Well there were a few clues, obviously the magazine letters, when we put them together were from various types of magazine. The gossip magazines, the OMG from 'OMG! Did you see' stuck out clearly. The style of magazines made us think we were looking for a woman. The knitting magazine and the fact that whoever it was had to be someone you knew and would see the effect the letters were having on you made us narrow the pool down again to the ladies at Bitch and Stitch." Rose elbowed Albert in the side. "Sorry Knit and Natter," he said blushing. Trish and Mary smiled. Rose took over.

"We were leaning towards 'Chelle for a while especially after her outburst outside the church but the gardening magazine threw out that theory. 'Chelle and Trace sharing a first floor flat with no garden seemed a bit odd that they would buy a gardening magazine."

"True," Trish replied, "almost everyone in that club has a garden though how did that get you to Joyce?"

"Well at that stage we almost considered Mary a suspect," Albert said. Mary and Trish both looked shocked. "Only because she met all the criteria on paper, woman, knitting, gossip mags, close friend and an avid gardener we found out. Also we knew there was something she was holding back, which we now know what that was of course. After thinking some more though it couldn't have been Mary. She has no reason to buy 'New You Skinny Moo'. Rose added, they all laughed.

"The key to Joyce though came when we looked at the dates the letters arrived. They were posted first class from this village only on Mondays and Wednesdays which meant whoever posted them knew they would arrive on Tuesdays and Thursdays." Albert raised his eyebrows towards Trish waiting for her to get his meaning.

"The days that Joyce works for us," she said as if it had just dawned on her. "She would collect the post first thing when she arrived in the morning and bring it straight to me, not Peter but to me. She wanted to see my reaction," Trish continued angry that she hadn't spotted this before. Her husband squeezed her hand sympathetically, he had felt guilt from his blindness that he refused to see anything but good in people even though he knew something about Joyce made his wife uncomfortable.

"That and the fact that we remembered Albert bumped into her outside the post office just as she was posting a letter on the Wednesday after we arrived, the day before you met us in the café with it. The one that mentioned Trace, and also that same day we saw her leaving your house looking rather smug," Rose said.

"She never smiles from what we have seen so that made us suspicious straight away," Albert said. The rest of the room nodded in agreement.

"We didn't have any real proof, all circumstantial, but bloody good circumstantial, so when it all got uncomfortable at Ponsonby's bash I took a chance and told you. I knew she had spent a lot of time at the hospital around the time of Maud's death and knew that you had mentioned seeing Ida there, it was a long shot but how else would she know about your past?" The room remained silent for a while, slurping their tea taking it all in.

"Well I don't know how to thank you both enough." The reverend spoke first. "You have helped give my wife back to me and helped catch an attempted murderer," he said forcing a smile. "I just don't know how I didn't see it, I'm such an idiot. My own brother," he continued sadly.

"You are not an idiot Peter," Trish spoke sternly. "You are a kind and gentle man who's only guilty of seeing and believing the best in people and don't you ever change that about yourself. Your ability to believe the good in people is what made me believe I could move on and fall in love and become the wife of the best vicar this village has ever known. None of this is your fault, you couldn't have known. None of us could." He blushed and smiled a grateful smile at Trish who smiled back, the first real smile they had seen from her since they arrived in Upper Wobble.

"And us," Mary joined in. "Thanks to you Ivan is behind bars and I finally feel free. "Anyway," she said standing up, "he can no longer control any of us. We can now hopefully all move on with our lives." The group did a mini toast with their teacups to this statement.

"I knew this day would come," George said quietly and with a tinge of sadness.

"What do you mean?" Mary said to him. George stood next to her and took her hands in his.

"You are free Mary," George said kindly. "Finally free. You can go wherever you want now, see the world, move to the seaside like you've always wanted. He can't hurt you anymore and you don't need to hide in this village with this old man anymore," he said sadly.

"What?" she replied. "What are you saying?"

"These years are the happiest of my entire life but I've been holding you back from doing what you really want and becoming what you always wanted, I always knew one day I'd have to let you go and live the life you really want. A woman as beautiful as you with such vibrancy, such life, shouldn't be stuck with an old man and a village tea shop." George was sad at the thought of losing Mary but he loved her so much he would not force her to live this life simply because at the time it was her only option. Now Ivan had been taken away he would let her go. She was silent for some time staring at him before walking over to him.

"You would really let me go?" she said cautiously. He took her hands in his and nodded at her faking a smile.

"I'd love to see more of the world. I have dreamed about it for so long." George looked at the ground glumly and nodded.

"But I'm not going anywhere without you." He looked up startled.

"George, I was his prisoner. You saved me from a life worse than death and I am forever in your debt but that is not why I have spent the last twenty odd years with you," she exclaimed. "I have been in love with you ever since you found me shivering and alone in the front garden at the shelter. You put your coat around me and for the first time I can remember a man's touch didn't make me flinch. I had never known such kindness, felt such warmth. In that moment I knew that my life wasn't over. You reawakened something in me I thought was long dead." A tear fell down Mary's cheek. "Our relationship George, this life, this isn't because I didn't have any other options." She was speaking loudly now, almost angry. "This is because I found my soul mate and fell in love with him." She placed a hand to his cheek. "Don't you ever, ever, ever think you are my plan B. And I don't care how old you are either you stupid man." Mary kissed her George firmly on the lips and they hugged each other so tightly. They were both laughing and crying at the same time now.

Rose and Albert looked on, Rose wiping a tear from her cheek as Albert squeezed her hand and did the manly blink away tears and start coughing trick. Life did have happy endings after all.

*

Albert and Rose were glad to get home. Albert didn't think he'd be able to cope with one more night falling down the step into the bedroom and the tiny uncomfortable Mad Cow bed. He'd miss the village and the free brandies, and the fact that they were getting paid to eat and drink but all in all it had been a successful first real case that they would never forget.

After wiping the slobbery kisses off themselves that they had got from Allan as they walked in the door they kissed their children.

Charlie had grabbed their bags and taken them upstairs. Poppy had given them the biggest squeeze of their lives. She had seen Ivan's photo in the newspaper and recognised him as the man with the limp who had left his wallet in the pub. Albert almost had a heart attack when he heard that Ivan had been anywhere near his daughter. Rose had calmed him down until she had popped out to collect something from her car and noticed some of her flower pots had been damaged and some flowers had snapped, then it was Albert's turn to calm her down.

Rose had come home to a nice pile of post, mainly bills, several Daily Wobbles, the most recent front page detailing Ivan's arrest as written by Lisa Von-Winkleknicker, who had indeed agreed to keep their names out of the paper. Also a little batch of Dear Doris letters, forwarded from her editor, one of which stood out as it had an Upper Wobble postmark. She opened it immediately.

Dear Doris

I am writing this letter not for advice but to say thank you.
Recently I had the pleasure of meeting you and Mr Doris and now our lives have changed forever.
You have helped to reveal both the best and worst of my friends and neighbours. Shown me who and what really counts and what doesn't.
You were able to reveal the hate mailer making my dear best friend's life a misery and even saved the life of another neighbour. You have helped put a murderer behind bars and given me back my life, for all of which I can never repay you enough.
Without your advice, perseverance and kindness the future for the entire village could have been tragically different.
If you are ever back in Upper Wobble we would love to see you.

Wishing you and your family all the best for the future.
Mary (Happy and content, Upper Wobble) xx

Rose had to blink back the tears again, handing the letter to Albert to read who in turn blinked back tears (or pretended to have something in his eye as per usual).

Poppy had put the kettle on and they all sat down at the family dining table to have a nice cup of tea when the door knocked. They all looked at each other hoping one of the others would answer it. Eventually Charlie decided to go.

Charlie returned with their old friend Dave Ramsbottom, looking very smart in his police uniform. The Nutters greeted their friend warmly. Dave and Albert shaking hands and Dave giving Rose a peck on the cheek.

"Thought you'd check we got back in one piece did you?" Albert said laughing. "Did you get the postcard I sent you?" he said giving Dave a nudge and a wink as Rose rolled her eyes. "Oh I hear the '3 brandies, 4 gin and tonics, 5 pints and we're anybody's Wibble Wobbles' came last." They all laughed, except Dave.

"Yeah that's right, we were rubbish without you." Dave smiled but there was something serious in his face.

"What is it Dave?" Albert asked. He could tell something was wrong. Dave sighed and rubbed his head.

"Got a bit of bad news I'm afraid," Dave said quietly. The Nutters looked at him expectantly.

"Well?" Albert said. "What is it?" he said almost angrily, Dave was starting to worry him now.

"It's Colin Killoran," Dave said, reluctantly.

"The killer clown?" Poppy said worryingly. Dave nodded.

"He was taken to hospital, had an epileptic fit, foaming at the mouth and everything," he continued.

"When he woke up, he managed to overpower his guard and assaulted two nurses and stabbed the police guard." Albert was shaking his head. He knew what was coming.

"He's escaped, Albert," Dave said. Rose and Poppy gasped simultaneously. "And according to evidence found in his cell, newspaper clippings, letters, drawings, even photographs," Dave paused, "he's coming for you."